## "Let's get in there and serve our guests," Adam said, holding a silver tray full of food.

He grinned, then headed through the swinging doors to the dining room. Stella grabbed another tray of food, thinking she liked the way he'd said "serve *our* guests."

*Don't be silly,* she admonished herself as she served the pleasantly surprised guests. These were loyal customers from past years, bless them. *He's just passing through. He just happened up when you were in a fix. He just happened up when you needed him most. And he'll be gone before you even miss him.* But the sweet smell of those incredible blueberry muffins made Stella hope Adam Callahan wouldn't be in too big a hurry to keep moving.

## LENORA WORTH

has written more than thirty books, most of those for Steeple Hill Books. She also works freelance for a local magazine, where she contributes monthly opinion columns, feature articles and social commentaries. She also wrote for five years for the local paper. Married to her high school sweetheart for thirty-two years, Lenora lives in Louisiana and has two grown children and a cat. She loves to read, take long walks and sit in her garden.

# Mountain Sanctuary
## Lenora Worth

Steeple
Hill®

Published by Steeple Hill Books™

STEEPLE HILL BOOKS

Steeple
Hill®

ISBN-13: 978-0-373-87473-6
ISBN-10:    0-373-87473-1

MOUNTAIN SANCTUARY

Copyright © 2008 by Lenora H. Nazworth

www.SteepleHill.com

**Printed in U.S.A.**

We continually remember before our God
and Father your work produced by faith,
your labor prompted by love and your endurance
inspired by hope in our Lord Jesus Christ.
—*1 Thessalonians* 1: 2–4

To Valerie Hansen, my treasured Arkansas friend!

# Chapter One

Adam Callahan slanted his head sideways so he could read the crooked sign in front of him.

Sanctuary House Inn Bed-and-Breakfast. Established 1888. Underneath the faded etched letters, a handwritten message announced Under New Management. Instead of a No Vacancy sign, someone had written—in what looked a child's scribblings—Lots Of Vacancies.

Well, he needed a bed and he needed breakfast. And this was apparently the last place in Hot Springs, Arkansas, that had both. Just his luck that he'd come rolling into town during some sort of art festival. Every hotel and bed-and-breakfast in Hot Springs and the surroundings areas of Lake Hamilton and Lake Catherine was booked solid for the next three days.

Except this one.

"Lots of vacancies," Adam said out loud as he straightened his head, the tight muscles in his neck reminding him why he'd left New Orleans in the first place.

"I need to rest," he said as he headed up the cracked, aged bricks of what once must have been a carriage drive. Looking up at the Gothic-like, Victorian-style turreted house with the peeling white paint and the broken green shutters, Adam wondered if he'd find any rest here. In the first light of an unforgiving yellow-gold dawn, the old house had the lost, forlorn look of a granny woman with dementia.

Adam could identify with that feeling. He'd been traveling all night and was bone weary. But he'd felt lost and forlorn for months now, his gut twisting with an emptiness that food couldn't fill. He also felt as if he'd been wandering in the wilderness for forty days, confused and dazed, after all the anguish he'd seen in his ten years as a police officer in New Orleans.

But you resigned from the force, he reminded himself, his gaze taking in the dead blossoms on the geraniums sitting in cracked pots by the side entrance to the B and B. The once-red blooms looked as burned-out and lifeless as Adam felt right now. With automatic precision, he reached down and plucked a few of the dried-up red blooms. Then he caught himself and stopped. He just needed sleep. Lots of sleep.

He'd just put one booted foot on the lopsided wooden steps, when he heard weeping coming from the open window right next to the porch.

Startled, Adam pivoted off the porch steps to stare into the long, wide window. The sight he saw immediately caught his attention and made him forget he was tired and sleepy.

A petite woman with waist-length, flowing strawberry-blond hair stood at the aged butcher-block table in the middle of the long, narrow kitchen, her hands covering her face as she leaned her head over and sobbed openly. The woman wore a flowery, gauzy dress covered by a smudged white apron that had so many ruffles they seemed to over-power both the dress and the woman wearing it. The smell of something burning caused Adam to glance from the distraught woman to the smoke coming out of the ancient six-burner stove sitting haphazardly against one wall. The woman seemed to be ignoring the smoke, but Adam saw a burned batch of what once must have been muffins spilled out on parchment paper on the messy butcher-block table. As he watched, the woman wiped at her eyes, then picked up one of the charred muffins and threw it across the kitchen, causing dishes to rattle in the wide, deep white porcelain sink.

Then she burst into tears again.

Which caused all of Adam's ingrained protective instincts to kick into overdrive, even while the practical part of his brain warned him in flashing, glaring banners to just turn around and keep walking.

"Excuse me," he heard himself saying into the window. "Uh, ma'am, could I possibly get a room?" Then, because he just couldn't stop himself, he added, "And is there anything I can do to help you?"

The sound of his voice caused the woman to look up in surprise, her expression changing from disturbed to mortified as she glared at Adam through the window. "What?"

"I need a place to stay," Adam said, his tone gentle now. "Can I come in?"

"Do you know how to make blueberry muffins?" the woman asked on a loud sniff, her daring expression telling him this might be the deal breaker.

"I sure do," he said with a soft smile. "I happen to make the best blueberry muffins this side of the Mason-Dixon line."

"You're teasing me, right?" she asked, tossing her long wavy hair back over her shoulder, her brilliant green eyes flashing. "And, mister, I am in no mood to be teased this morning."

"I'm not teasing," Adam replied, determination making him want to win entry into this strange, intriguing house so he could find out what was the matter with this strange, intriguing woman. "I was a cook in the navy. And on the police force back in New Orleans, I was the unofficial designated cook for all of our get-togethers. I did all the cooking for the guys—" He stopped, remembering cookouts and crawfish boils back on the bayou. "I can make muffins," he said, his tone turning blunt and businesslike as he shoved the memories away. "But first, you have to let me in. Oh, and you might want to check on whatever's in the oven."

At that, she let out a wail and rushed to the oven, then opened it to let out even more smoke. Shouting to Adam over her shoulder, she said, "C'mon on in. And hurry."

Adam didn't waste time getting there. He rushed up onto the side porch, found the door unlocked and entered, the big stained glass door squeaking his arrival.

A small boy wearing action-figure-embellished pajamas stood waiting for him, his hair the same thick strawberry-blond color of the woman's. The boy slanted big hazel eyes underneath long bangs, then flapped his hands in the air. "Wow, am I glad to see you. This is the third batch she's tried this morning, and most of our visitors have done left and gone to get a sausage biscuit out on the highway."

Adam had to chuckle at the kid's dead-serious expression. "And just who are you?"

"Kyle Watson Forsythe," the boy said, extending a hand in a very grown-up manner. "I'm trying to help my mom. But she says this place is nothing but a big, ol' money pit and she wishes she'd never in-hair-it-ted it in the first place."

Adam wondered what else the kid, who looked to be around six or seven, had learned from his mama, but he refrained from asking that right now. "Show me the way to the kitchen, son," he said in his best cop voice, his instincts on full alert.

The boy rubbed his nose, then pointed. "Down that hallway to the right." He pointed again, his expression bordering on panic. "She thinks the stove is messed up."

"Thanks." Adam dropped his leather duffel bag onto the hardwood floor and stalked across the formal Victorian parlor toward the kitchen and the sobbing woman.

Stella's head came up at the swishing of the swinging door, her mind numb with failure and a definite lack of faith. Everyone had assured her that running this place would be an ideal job for her since she was organized to a fault and had a good business head. They said the Sanctuary practically took care of itself. Well, they had all been somewhat misinformed. And she'd been gullible and crazy to think she could do this on her own. Wishing the older couple that had helped her mother hadn't retired to Branson, Stella squared her shoulders and took a deep breath as she waited for the muffin man.

She'd take whatever help she could find, including help from a perfect stranger.

The man who came barreling into the kitchen seemed to fill the vast space with his very presence, causing Stella to inhale the leftover sob she'd been about to emit into the air. Wiping her eyes with one of the annoying frilly ruffles of her dead mother's apron, Stella tried to focus on this interesting person who'd apparently come to her rescue.

He was tall, but not too tall. His hair was clipped and edged into brittle brown tufts across his forehead and around his ears. His eyes, wide and hesitant right now, were a rich grayish blue. But it was his face that held Stella's attention. His face looked as worn and aged as the masculine tan wallpaper in her daddy's study across the hallway. It was a face etched in hard living, all planes and angles, all rough male, muscular and scarred. This man, whoever he was, sure didn't look like someone who could make blueberry muffins. More like he could take down a band of ragamuffins with one strong-armed swipe.

"Did you say the navy?" she asked, dumbfounded.

"Yeah, two tours of duty. Then ten years on the police force in New Orleans. I'm retired now."

The way he said that made Stella think it might not have been a voluntary retirement. "Is it still bad from the storms down there?" she asked, not one for making small talk.

"As bad as things can get and then some, but I still love the place." He opened the refrigerator and found the fresh blueberries, then grabbed a mixing bowl from the ones stacked along an open bottom shelf underneath the butcher block. "Flour?"

Stella pointed to the tin canister sitting on the counter. "I have the recipe—"

"Don't need it. I have my own recipe." He tapped his forehead. "Right here."

She leaned across the counter. "That's real nice, but do you have a way of fixing an oven that refuses to cook at the correct temperature? I'm pretty sure the thermostat has gone haywire."

He opened the door of the oven. "I think I see the problem, but it'll have to cool down before I can get in there and fix it. Do you have a microwave or a toaster oven?"

She nodded. "But—"

"I know how to make microwave muffins."

"Amazing," Stella said through a sniff. "Uh, what's your name?"

"Adam," he said, eyeballing flour into the bowl. "Adam Callahan. And you?"

"Stella Forsythe."

"Nice to meet you, Stella." Then he motioned with his head toward the refrigerator. "I need about two eggs."

She managed to find him "about two" eggs and "about a half cup" of oil and several other ingredients he called for in precise order. Then she stood back and watched as he went to work, his gray gaze centered on the creamy mixture inside the big white bowl.

"Do you need the mixer?" she asked.

"Nope." He floured the blueberries, then whipped them right into the mix, lifting an eyebrow toward her. "But I do need a clean muffin pan. One that works in the microwave."

Stella scrambled to find a pan that wasn't coated with burned muffin remains. "I have this plastic one I use in there. Should I grease it?"

"Yeah. Grease and a little flour all over."

She did as he told her, glad the splotchy red patches she always got along her neck and throat whenever she was under emotional stress had seemed to settle down into just freckles now. She hated getting all splotchy, but today had been a triple splotchy day, and it wasn't even 7:00 a.m. yet.

"I'd planned an egg casserole, too," she told him as he put the muffins into the microwave. "But—"

"Give me the ingredients," he told her, his hands on his hips, a wet, white dish towel with tiny daisies on its hem thrown across his broad shoulder.

Stella moved like a sleepwalker, gathering ham and eggs, cheese and bread, her thoughts running together mumbo jumbo. *Lord, how did I get so lucky?* she asked the heavens in a silent prayer of thanks. *Dear God, did You finally hear my pleas?* The smell of blueberry muffins answered her, sweet and plump and intoxicating.

In minutes, the man had created a big glass Pyrex dish full of the breakfast-casserole concoction, adding a sprinkle of nutmeg to the top to make it look pretty. After the muffins were done, he shoved that into the microwave, then he meticulously went about tidying up the kitchen, stopping here and there to grunt out questions to Stella.

"How old's your boy?"

"Six."

"How long you been in Hot Springs?"

"About two months."

"What happened with the muffins this morning?"

"I don't know how to cook very well and the oven doesn't, either."

"Why is this place such a mess?"

"Because of the oven. I got backed up with the first batch of muffins, so I tried another one. Things went downhill from there."

About forty minutes and twenty questions later, the casserole bubbled its way to perfection. Announcing it almost done, he turned back to Stella. "How many?"

"How many what?"

"How many people are you expecting for breakfast?"

A little voice from the corner of the room shouted out. "We only got about four people waiting in the parlor, Mama. The rest left."

Stella glanced over at her son. "Oh, Kylie, why are you still in your pajamas?" She'd told him to get dressed, but the boy had a mind of his own.

Kyle grinned, showing the gap where he'd lost two teeth. "I was just talking to everyone."

The boy could talk, no doubt about that. "Run on up and get dressed and then you can eat. I'll take care of our guests." Since his father had died, Kyle somehow thought he had to be the man of the house. That realization brought more tears to her eyes, but Stella held this batch of sobs back for her son's sake. "Thank you, honey, for entertaining our guests. You can tell them to meet us in the dining room. Breakfast will soon be served."

"Did this man cook all that food?" Kyle asked, clearly impressed.

Stella sent a shy glance toward the big man washing dishes. "He sure did."

"Sweet," Kyle said, his eyes bright with unbridled delight. "I'm starving to death." Then he looked back toward Stella, his big brown eyes breaking her heart with love. "Can I go get Papa?"

"Yes, go tell Papa to come and get it while it's hot."

Kyle grinned. "Ain't he gonna be surprised?"

Stella smiled. Answering her son with an example of correct English, she said, "Yes, Papa certainly is going to be surprised. Not *ain't gonna.*"

"Whatever," Kyle said with kid practicality. "He ain't gonna believe his eyes, that's for sure."

Stella shook her head, then tossed her hair back.

Adam eyed her over his shoulder. "He's a handful, I reckon."

"You can say that again."

"What's your husband do?"

"He's dead."

"I'm sorry."

"Don't be. He's probably better off that way. And I know we're better off for it."

Realizing the man was staring at her with such intensity it bordered on shock, Stella waved a hand in the air. "I shouldn't have said that. Lawrence was a no-good, cheating, drinking vagrant who pretty much robbed me blind, but I guess he had a soul. Or at least I hope so, anyway, for Kyle's sake. He had a bad wreck on I-30 one rainy Saturday night about a year ago. Wrapped his souped-up Mustang around a steel pole on an embankment. And that was that."

"Is that why you moved here?"

"No." She wondered just when he'd get enough and leave. Everybody usually did. "I moved here af-

ter my mother died last year. This was her house."
She shrugged. "I mean, she lived here, but somebody ran the place for her. She spent most of her
time out back in the studio. She was…an artist."

He nodded at that, his expression blank as he
rinsed a now-scrubbed muffin pan. "And Papa?"

Well, the man didn't miss a thing. Figured, him
being a cop. Always aware of his surroundings, she
reasoned. She knew how cops operated, since her
dearly departed husband had several run-ins with
the law over the years she'd been with him. "Papa
is my daddy, Watson Clark. Everyone calls him
Wally, though. My mother left him when I was ten,
but they never divorced. After she died, I brought
him here to live with us and help out. But he can't
do a whole lot. He has a lot of health problems."

She finished wiping down the counter, then prepared the plates for the guests, careful to make sure
each plate was distinctively different in style and
pattern, just to mix things up. She'd read somewhere that it was okay to do that, and besides, she
didn't really care about proper etiquette at this point.

"Got any fruit?" Adam asked over her shoulder, causing her to almost drop a delicate blue-
etched plate.

"In the refrigerator. Strawberries, I think. And
maybe some grapes."

"We'll add a few bites to each serving," Adam

said, already digging through the stuffed refrigerator. "You need to clean this thing out."

"I'll get to it," Stella said, thinking one day she'd get to every little thing around here. "Soon."

"Let's get in there and serve our guests," Adam said, holding a silver tray full of food in his hands. "Got the coffee ready?"

"Yes, I do know how to make coffee at least." Then she winced. "Well, you might want to test it before we take it out."

"I think I just might."

He grinned, then headed through the swinging doors to the dining room. Stella grabbed another tray of food, thinking she liked the way he'd said "serve our guests."

Don't be silly, she admonished as she served the pleasantly surprised guests who were loyal customers from past years, bless them. He's just passing through. He just happened up when you were in a fix. He just happened up when you needed him the most. And he'll be gone before you even miss him. But the sweet smell of those incredible blueberry muffins made Stella hope Adam Callahan wouldn't be in too big of a hurry to keep moving.

# Chapter Two

"So...can I get my room now?"

Adam stood in the kitchen with Stella, watching as she put away the last of the breakfast dishes. The meal had been a success. The older couple from Florida and the honeymooners from Texas had all raved about the breakfast, all four of them fascinated and in awe as they asked Stella over and over how she'd pulled it off.

"First breakfast we've had in two days that wasn't either burned or raw," Mr Gilchrest said with a wink. "Stella, did you find a new cookbook somewhere?"

"No, just a new friend," Stella told the senior citizen, her eyes glowing with pride while her father and her son looked on with that same pride.

"Are you gonna keep him?" Joyce Gilchrest asked, her hazel eyes full of curiosity as she gave Adam the once-over.

Stella laughed and tossed her incredible hair. "I'm sure gonna give him that room he came looking for, you can count on that. Adam has to be exhausted after whipping up this great breakfast so lickety-split."

Joyce smiled over at Adam. "We've been coming here every spring for the last ten years. We miss Estelle, but we love Stella just about as much as we loved her mother. So we came back this year to lend her our support."

"It's mighty nice of you to be that loyal," Adam said.

"We love it here," Joyce replied. "I think you will, too. Don't you think so, Wally?"

Wally Clark gave Adam a long appraising look that was part gratitude and part protectiveness. Stella's father was a quiet man, unassuming and undemanding, but Adam sensed a steel-encased dignity behind the calm, stoic exterior.

"Hot Springs—you either love it or hate it," Wally replied, his smile serene.

"I liked those muffins," Kyle offered up, his big eyes solemn. "But not the burned ones."

"Kylie, finish your breakfast," Stella said, turning red in the face. But she sent her son a sweet smile, all the same.

The honeymooners sitting across the dining room cooed and grinned, obviously too in love to expect anyone else to have problems in this life. "It was good," the pretty blonde said, smiling over at her doting husband. "But then, I can hardly remember any of the meals anyway. We're having so much fun."

"I sure remember 'em," Mr. Gilchrest replied with a grimace. "Had indigestion to remind me." He chuckled then nodded toward Stella. "But I have very high hopes for our Stella. She's gonna turn this place into a showcase one day."

Adam watched as Stella basked in the compliments. "This place has a lot of potential," he said, sending her his own smile of confidence. "And so does the hostess."

Stella waved a hand in the air in dismissal. "Okay, now, don't go giving me a big head. I still got a lot to learn. And the first rule—hire good help."

"Amen," Mr. Gilchrest said, lifting his coffee cup.

They all laughed out loud at that, including Adam.

Now that everyone had been fed, and the guests had headed out to the festival, Stella bobbed her head in response to Adam's question, her long hair cascading over her shoulder. "Papa's putting fresh sheets on the downstairs bedroom right across from the parlor. It's a smaller room near our private quarters, but it's usually nice and quiet toward the front of the house. And we have a creditable library down there, too, if you like to read."

Adam lifted his head. "And far enough away from the stove?" At her confused look, he added, "Smoke."

"Funny." Then she looked down at the now-polished and shining butcher-block counter. "I want to thank you, Adam. I don't know what I would have done this morning if you hadn't come along. I'm good at multitasking, so I usually have things under control, but I might have taken on too much with this place. I'm not normally so emotional, but well…it just all hit me at once this morning. A lot has gone wrong around here since I took over. But I'm determined to make it work."

Adam could see that although she was pretty and petite, Stella Forsythe seemed to be carrying the weight of the world on her tiny shoulders. "You're in a tough spot," he said. "We just have to figure how to get you out of it."

"If I knew what I was doing, that might help," she said with a self-deprecating snort. "My mother left me this place, and at first, I saw it as a new beginning. I'd been living hand to mouth up in Little Rock, working odds jobs here and there just to keep Kyle fed and clothed." She shrugged, started gathering up dish towels. "My mother and I weren't exactly close. She left us when I was young and I never forgave her. So I was shocked when I found out I'd inherited this old place. Shocked and amazed."

She glanced around, her green eyes lifting

toward the high ceiling of the kitchen. "I used to dream of living here with her. I got to visit her during the summer, but I wanted to live here all the time, with both my parents. My dad did the best he could, working hard to raise me, sending me to school, cooking dinner for us at night, helping me with my homework. But...I guess I needed my mama, too. That's why I was crying this morning. I needed my mama."

Adam looked down at the aged wooden floor where the slant in the boards met in the middle of the big room with a soft sag. "That had to be tough. Why didn't you live with her? I mean, fathers rarely win custody of a child."

Stella let out a soft chuckle, then shook her head. "My family doesn't go by the book on such things. They never divorced, never consulted any lawyers. They just kind of agreed that I'd stay with Daddy. You see, he was the more solid of the two." She started walking toward the little laundry room just off the kitchen. "My mother's only passion was her art. She could paint a pretty picture, but she didn't have a pretty life."

Adam didn't question her anymore. She looked drained, washed out, defeated. "Uh...I guess I'll go get a shower and some sleep." At her nod, he stopped. "Stella, maybe we could negotiate an arrangement of sorts."

She lifted her slanted brows. "What kind of arrangement?"

The question was asked with a not-so-subtle suspicion, as if she'd made arrangements before and lived to regret them.

"In exchange for room and board, I could help out around here for a while. Fix things up, cook. I'm good at things like that—you know, fixing up, cleaning up and cooking."

Adam hated the plea in his voice, but he didn't want to leave the Sanctuary Inn just yet. Something about the needy old house had captivated him. Or maybe it was something about the need he saw in the woman standing beside him that had captivated him. Besides, he wasn't intent on going anyplace in a hurry. He'd come here to get as far away as possible from his past and his old life. Why not stay awhile and just…rest?

Stella looked at him as if he might be crazy, her eyes going wide, her mouth opening and then closing. "You'd be willing to do all that just for a place to sleep?"

"Sure. Don't get me wrong. I'm not destitute. But I am on a budget, being retired and all. And it'd just be until I can find…until I can decide what to do next."

She stood with her foot propped against the partially open door to the laundry room, the bundle of towels in her hands. "I'll have to discuss it with Papa and Kyle, but I think we might be able to work something out. I mean, if you can make meals like the one you made this morning and help me get this place back into shape, well, who am I to turn you away?"

"I can fix that oven, too," he reminded her. "Easy."

"Then you've got a job." She named her terms. "Room and board—and a weekly salary—I insist on paying you for your time and trouble." She told him what the last maintenance man got paid. "Is that reasonable?"

"More than reasonable. Thank you," Adam said, no other words available. It had been a long time since anyone had just accepted him. But then, he figured Stella had just about reached the end of the road, same as he had. "I'm going to my room now. I guess I'll see you later."

"Yes, later," she said, her expression puzzled and questioning. She turned to head into the laundry room, then whirled back around. "Adam?"

"Hmm?"

"Why are you here?"

Adam braced one hand on the swinging door opposite her, wondering how to answer that very loaded question. "It's the first place I saw that had a vacancy," he said. "Seemed like a good place to lay my head." And before she could question him again, he turned and went through the swinging door, the *swish, swish* of it moving behind him, sending little currents of air chasing at his retreating back.

Stella went about the business of getting all the linens washed. This work she didn't mind so much. This work had meaning. Washing away the old, bringing out the fresh and clean. She liked to fold the sheets and towels just out of the dryer, the smell of sunshine and tropical breezes making her put her nose to the crisp white linens.

At least her mother had had the good sense to buy nice linens. Or maybe it had been Mrs. Ebard. Mrs. Ebard and her husband had managed the Sanctuary up until the day Stella had taken over. Tired and old and cranky, the married couple couldn't wait to leave and be done with the falling-down old house. Stella remembered Louise Ebard's words to her the day she'd called to tell Stella that Estelle Forsythe had died.

"She just went to sleep and never woke up. Heart attack. At fifty-five. And her a little skinny thing, at that. 'Course, it might have been the smoking and drinking or the late nights out in that studio, who knows." After much sniffing and crying, Mrs. Ebard had added, "She wanted you to have the inn, honey. Told me long ago—that's in her will. But I have to tell you, things are bad here. It's a bit run-down. We don't get many visitors except the ones that have been coming here for years. Just the regulars or the occasional traveler who can't find anything better. I still cook and Ralph works on the yard and house, but we can't keep at this anymore. It's just bad."

"Really bad," Stella said now, hearing the sound of her son's laughter out in the back garden. Her daddy was out there with Kyle, trying to clip the wisteria back before it took over the studio. Her mother had loved wisteria. But as beautiful as the purple, scented blossoms were this time of year, Stella knew even wisteria, left untamed, eventually suffocated everything in its path. The same way her mother had filled a room and suffocated everyone and everything in it, taking over, demanding, manipulating, the sweet scent of her perfume mixed with the charcoal smell of cigarettes wafting through the air until Stella would almost choke with the pain and grief of not measuring up, of not understanding that her mother was both brilliant and a bit mad.

"Flighty." That's what her father had called his Estelle. Flighty and scatterbrained and tormented and talented. Not a woman made for maternal instincts, not a woman made to stay with one man. Not a woman to want her only daughter to bother her when she was working. One simple, hardworking man and one small, scared little girl, left behind, with only the scent of wisteria to comfort them.

And yet, they'd both willingly come here to the

home where the woman they'd loved had lived alone amongst strangers. And died alone, all of her guests gone. Maybe they were each hoping to catch a bit of Estelle's elusive spirit, to be near the places she'd been near, to touch the things she'd touched.

Stella hoped her father tamed that wisteria vine, once and for all. And she had to wonder for the hundredth time *why* she'd even bothered coming here. Did she want to be reminded of all that her mother had given up in order to have her freedom, her art? Did she want to be here so she could remember, or had she brought her son and her father here to start over, to forget?

Daddy would tell her to put her trust in God. Daddy was a good, Christian man with a solid work ethic, but he'd had his heart broken long ago. Had that been a part of God's grand plan for him?

Stubbornly, Stella put her nose to a white lace-trimmed pillowcase, closing her eyes to take in the freshness of it. New, clean, washed. She prayed God would one day make her feel that way. And then she thought about Adam Callahan and wondered what his story was. What was he running from, to come here to this sad old house, to ask to be able to stay here? He'd called the Sanctuary a good place to lay his head. Maybe he was right there. It certainly was a place for confused, wayward travelers. Even if some of those travelers thought they were coming home.

"Mama, why you got your nose in that pillow cover?"

Her son's words jarred Stella out of her musings. Opening her eyes, she tried to focus. "Oh, I was just enjoying the nice smell."

"Papa and me are thirsty. He sent me for lemonade. That store-bought stuff is pretty good. Papa said we can keep buying it, since the last time we tried to make it fresh, you poured the juice down the drain by accident."

Stella remembered. Five crushed lemon rinds and no juice to show for it, since she'd somehow managed to pour out the juice instead of the rinds. "I kind of got things backward that day, didn't I?"

Kyle grinned. "It's okay. The kind we get at the store is powdery and already squeezed."

Stella looked down at her child, her heart unfolding toward him with a maternal surge of hope and pride. She loved her son, had loved him enough to fight for him, and she couldn't imagine leaving him, ever. His daddy had been bad to the bone, but so good-looking and persuasive, so intense, that Stella had somehow overlooked that one big flaw. Stella had married Lawrence Forsythe on an impulsive whim, tinged with a passionate need to love and be loved.

But their son, ah, their son was priceless, as perfect and pure as a fine piece of porcelain. As sturdy and strong as the timbers in this old house. He'd had to grow up too fast after his father's death, but soon Kyle would have better. Kyle would survive and thrive, because Stella had her father here to guide him. And in spite of her own bent toward wanting to paint pretty pictures on everything from benches to teacups, Stella had to be practical and sure. She had to work to get this place back up and running. For Kyle's sake. She wanted to be the one to take care of her son, not the other way around.

Kyle had a keen sense of responsibility. Her father called him an old soul. But Stella didn't want him to miss out on just being a child. She'd had to grow up too quickly in order to take care of her mother at times. Kyle wouldn't have to do that.

And that meant she certainly wouldn't look a gift horse in the mouth and turn him away. Adam Callahan had offered to help out. Stella, being practical in spite of her artistic side, aimed to take him up on that offer. Just as soon as she explained things to her father and her son, of course.

Adam heard laughter. Maybe he was dreaming, but the sound brought him a kind of gentle peace. The laughter floated through his subconscious mind, reminding him of lazy days spent fishing with his father and brothers out on the bayou, of time spent riding the big boat out on Lake Pontchartrain, good times. Happy times. Laughter.

He woke with a start, wondering where he was. He was hot and sweaty, his brow wet, his pulse pounding. Lifting his head, he slowly glanced around the darkened room, his gaze taking in the shiny mahogany armoire, the old-fashioned washstand with the white bowl and pitcher, the four-poster bed with the soft, fresh sheets and the rose-quilted cover. Sanctuary.

He was at the Sanctuary House Inn in Hot Springs, Arkansas. Hundred of miles away from New Orleans. A million miles away from his past. Had he come far enough?

Adam got up and took a long shower, enjoying the soft spray as he reminded himself to check the pressure later. The old claw-foot bathtub was respectable, even if it was ancient, but the shower could use a few tweaks. Maybe he'd install one of those fancy newfangled showerheads. That would certainly be a plus for guests.

He got dressed, his mind already at work as he made a mental note of all the things he'd noticed around this place that needed to be fixed. Shutters that needed to be repaired and repainted. Porch steps that needed to be straightened and steadied. Rugs cleaned, trees trimmed.

He was already out in the hallway across from the dark paneled library when it hit him that somehow in the space of about six hours and several sweet dreams, he'd made a commitment to a place he didn't even know. And to a woman he surely didn't even begin to understand. Not a good idea. Not good at all. What if things became all tangled, like the ivy vine growing down on the sign post? He might just have to tell Stella that he'd changed his mind, that he couldn't stay after all.

But then, Adam came down the steps leading to the back gardens and stopped, his heart slamming against his chest, his breath halting in his lungs as he watched the scene playing out before him.

Mr. Clark sat in an old rusty wrought iron lawn chair, gently rocking it back and forth, while Stella and Kyle laughed and moved around in the un-mowed wildflower clusters at the back end of the long, wide yard. They were playing ring-around-the-rosy. The afternoon sun surged around them like a halo, all bright and white and piercing. Kyle looked up, giggling, as his mother held his hands, skipping in a circle with him, her long, bright hair falling down toward the floral skirt of her dress. Stella threw her head back, laughing, teasing, while Kyle squealed with delight as they swirled faster and faster in the red clovers and tiny wild onion flowers, daffodils and black-eyed Susans frolicking in the wind right in step with them.

Adam held on to the porch rail, his eyes tightening against the too-bright swell of emotions filling his insides. Once long ago, he'd dreamed of just such a picture in his own life. But his job had eaten away at any intimacy, any type of happiness he might have found. He'd loved and left a lot of women, or more likely, they'd loved him and he'd left them. The job had always taken what little soul he had to give. And in the end, the job had taken all of him, all of his strength, all of his energy, all of his dreams. Adam had been too involved in real life to have any dreams in his own life.

But standing here now, watching the sweetness of a simple spring afternoon, hearing the drone of bumblebees on the rosebushes and the fussing and chirping of mockingbirds up in the big old live oak just beyond the house, and seeing this woman and her child playing with joy and abandon in the flower-filled yard of an old house that seemed to sigh in its contentment, Adam thought again about his dreams. And his torments. And he wished he could play with them, wished he could laugh out loud again.

But he couldn't move. So he just stood there, watching, observing, with all of his cop instincts on full-throttle warning, while his heart sent out a warning of its own. Turn away, it told him inside each erratic beat. Don't dream. It hurts too much. But he couldn't turn away. He just couldn't. The image of Stella and Kyle laughing and playing would stay with him for a very long time to come, like a faded picture held just out of his reach, a sweet reminder of all that was good and great in life. A reminder of all that he would never have.

Then Stella stopped skipping and fell down into the wildflowers, giggling as Kyle fell with her. She lifted her head, taking a breath, and saw Adam standing there. Her eyes held his, a soft surprised smile on her pink lips.

And she called out to him. "Adam, come and join us."

Adam Callahan closed his eyes, images of death and crime, of drugs and killers and abuse and anger, moving through his tired, jaded brain to remind him that he'd dropped out of life. He'd once been a good cop. But then, he'd done something to change all of that. It didn't matter that he was only trying to save a family member, it was still wrong. So wrong that Adam hadn't used good judgment. Now he was paying for that with this self-imposed exile.

"Adam?"

Stella's soft, melodious call seemed to push away all the dark-edged ugliness he'd seen in his head. Adam opened his eyes, smiled at her, then slowly starting walking through the overgrown garden toward the source of all that laughter and sunshine.

# *Chapter Three*

The next day, Adam stood on a ladder on the side of the house, working on putting a decrepit shutter back in place. His goal for today was to get all the shutters cleaned, repaired and lined up straight, so he could decide how to paint the old house. He'd have to take them all down to really clean and paint them, but for now just setting them straight would have to do. He'd do some scraping and cleaning, and some sandblasting before he could actually worry about a new paint job. That and the fact that Stella didn't have a whole lot of money for paint, meant Adam might be here a little longer than he'd originally planned.

But then, he reminded himself as green paint flecks showered his head, he hadn't really had an original plan.

He'd just wanted to keep moving, until he'd arrived here. And now, the lovely owner of this inn and her family had talked it over and had all agreed to let Adam stay here for a while. He couldn't say no to that kind of appreciation, that kind of tight-knit acceptance.

As if reading his thoughts, Kyle appeared next to the camellia bush near the window. "I sure am glad we voted to keep you, Mr. Adam."

Adam grinned down at the energetic little boy. "Me, too, Kyle. It's nice to have something to occupy my time while I'm here."

Kyle bobbed his head, ran a dirty hand across his nose. "Mama said you needed a place to sleep, and I can be your friend."

"I did need a place to sleep, and I sure could use a friend," Adam replied, careful to keep his tone even and unassuming. This little boy and his pretty mama were a bit too astute. Adam had come on this trek seeking seclusion and time to relax and get his head straight. If he got too involved with Kyle and Stella, he might not reach any of those goals. But his couple of days here so far had been relaxing, in spite of the work that running a bed-and-breakfast demanded. And he liked that right now. He liked staying busy in a mindless sort of way that didn't require guns and handcuffs or criminals and lost souls. "So you think I need a friend, huh?"

"Yep. My mama said she reckoned you were hurting real bad." He shrugged. "What'd cha do, scrape your knee or something like that?"

Adam lowered his head to stare down at the cute little boy, wishing he still had such an innocent, wise heart. "Yeah, something like that."

Kyle jumped as the door to the back porch slammed. Stella came down the stairs, her long blue-and-white paisley skirt swirling around her legs. "Kyle Watson Forsythe, are you talking this man's poor head off again?"

Kyle squinted, then gave Adam a hard stare. "He's still got his head, silly."

"I'll silly you if you don't get inside and eat your peanut butter and jelly sandwich," Stella retorted, her green eyes full of mirth. "C'mon now."

"Are we going to the festival later, like you promised?" Kyle asked, dragging his sneakered feet until she replied.

"Yes, but only if you pick up your toys and help Papa empty the trash."

"Yes, ma'am." Kyle started for the door, then turned, his hands on his hips. "Hey, Mr. Adam, you coming to the festival with us?"

Adam shot a glance toward Stella, to see how she might react to this gracious invitation. She looked embarrassed, confused and unsure. But she gave him a quick little smile. "You're welcome to come."

He doubted that, but he played along. "Are you sure?"

"We're as sure as corn shucks," Kyle replied, bobbing his head.

"Get inside," Stella said, pointing a finger toward the kitchen. "Now."

Adam shook his head, then grinned as the back door slammed. "He's a pistol."

"Tell me." Stella plopped down on the steps to stare up at him. "He was born an old soul, according to my daddy. Much too wise for his young years." She surveyed his work for a minute. "How's it coming with the windows and shutters?"

Adam let out a mock groan. "Well, considering there are about twenty-six shutters on this house, I'd say it's coming along very slowly. Should take a few days, at least, to do it right."

"So you might just need a break later this afternoon?"

Adam eyed his progress so far. He'd managed to get about six shutters cleaned off, scraped and hinged back into place and the day was already half-done. "I just might at that."

Stella got up, tossed her long ponytail over her shoulder. "Well, Rome wasn't built in a day. You don't have to do everything at once."

Adam finished his work, then came down the rickety ladder to face her. "I've got it all worked out.

Shutters and windows cleaned and fixed first. Then scraping and sanding these old boards for some primer. Then a whole new paint job—"

Stella held up a hand. "You're talking a lot of money."

"I know. But I can find discount paint on the Internet."

"You can?"

"Sure. And speaking of that, do you have a Web site? You need one, you know, to attract customers."

Stella backed up, stared at him. "You sure move fast."

Adam thought he'd been standing still long enough. Or at least it felt that way now that he had something to focus on. The house, he reminded himself, not the woman. "Just trying to get things lined up. I mean, if you still want me to stay and help you out."

"Oh, I'd like that, but I don't have the money for a major renovation. I'll just be happy that all the shutters are stable and secure again."

He nodded, then looked down at his work boots. "When I get my mind set on a thing, I can be a steamroller at times."

She looked skeptical and full of wonder, as if she wished she could figure him out. "Really now?"

He grinned at the teasing light in her eyes. "Okay,

I can be a real pain at times. But that's just my nature. I like to stay busy and I like things in order."

Stella put a hand in the air. "We might be in trouble then. I'm slow and steady and I used to be efficient and organized. But I'm still learning this business." Then she looked out toward the wisteria wrapping around the garage. "Of course, that's why you found me burning muffins the other day. I got so overwhelmed, I let things slide. Maybe I do need to be more organized, considering this place is my only livelihood now. Starting with a Web site. But one thing at a time, Callahan, okay?"

Adam took that declaration in stride. "I understand. In other words, I don't need to be rushing you, right?"

She shrugged, glanced down at the wilted petunias by the back steps. "No, no. Somebody sure needs to set me on the right path. I know it looks bad around here, but I have every intention of getting this place back up and running. Somehow, my mother managed to make a living between the inn and her art. Of course, she did have good help." Then she sank back down on the steps. "I'm just not quite sure how *I'm* gonna do that. I like all of your ideas, but I need to think them through. Make the right choices."

"Do you have any guests booked after the festival is over?" Adam asked as he sat down beside her, then started yanking weeds away from the steps. The two loyal couples who'd stayed to endure Stella's cooking would be checking out tomorrow.

"For the summer, you mean?"

He nodded. "That would be good, yes."

"Nobody next week." She looked out toward the big studio, her expression wistful. "We have a few reservations over the next few weeks. There's always some kind of festival going on downtown."

"Not quite as bad as I thought."

"I told you, I'm trying."

"I can see that. So let me help."

"What's in it for you?" she said, tossing her hair again, a spark of doubt flickering through her eyes. "You seem almost too good to be true. There's got to be a catch."

Adam let out a sigh. "No catch, and I'm not all that good. I told you, I just needed a place to—"

"To hide?" She gave him a green-eyed stare, her smile bittersweet. "You're hiding out, right?"

Adam shook his head, deciding he'd better just level with her. "No, not exactly. Look, I worked for the New Orleans Police Department for a long time. I've seen things, you know. Bad things. Things that make a man question his sanity and his faith. I had to walk away."

"Do you still have faith?"

Because the question seemed so important to

her, Adam knew the answer would be, too. "I have faith, yeah. I come from a good, solid family. My daddy taught all of us to never give up on God, no matter what."

"But your job made you doubt Him?"

"Him and everything else in life."

She braced her elbows on her knees, put her head in her hands, then looked out toward the wisteria vines again, her smile disappearing as fast as a dandelion's floating whiskers. "Well, take it from me, you can run but you can't hide—from your doubts, I mean. I doubt myself and God on a daily basis. But seems to me, things just keep on coming. Right now, I'm not on very good speaking terms with the Big Man."

"How do *you* keep going then?"

She smiled again, the lifting of her lips a sweet symbol of something Adam couldn't understand. "Kyle keeps me going. I have to remember Kyle. And my daddy. I love them both so much. And they've both been hurt and abandoned. I have to keep the faith for their sakes, at least." She shrugged. "In case you haven't noticed, my son tries very hard to be the mature one around here. He needs to be a kid again, before it's too late."

Adam looked over at her then, taking in the deep shimmer of her hair, the defiant tilt of her chin. He wondered about her hurts, her scars and her own lost childhood. "And what about for your sake?"

She turned her head to look at him, her eyes wide with bewilderment. "I guess I'm hoping some of their luster will rub off on me. You know, faith by association. I don't always practice what my daddy tries to preach, but it does sink in. And it sure couldn't hurt Kyle, right?"

He laughed. "Right. Couldn't hurt." Then he turned serious. "If you feel uncomfortable about me being here—"

"It's not that. It's just…I've never known a man other than my daddy who was as good as his word. Certainly not my dearly departed husband. And certainly not any of the many men my mother knew— according to rumors I'd hear from her staff now and then, at least. I guess it's not easy for me to take you at your word. And I can't take God at His word, either. I have to see something to believe it."

Adam could understand that notion. But he wanted her to understand him, to understand that he didn't know how to operate, except by the principles and standards he'd learned as a child. "My word is all I've got right now. And you have to believe me when I say that being here right now is the best thing for me. It's like therapy, only way less expensive."

"After New Orleans?"

"Yes, after New Orleans."

She gave him one of those long, big-eyed stares

again, but didn't press him for the details. "We do tend to take things in stride here. We're a lot more relaxed than the big city. We're as laid back as New Orleans, but in a different way."

"I like that." And he liked the way her vanilla-scented shampoo smelled, too, he reasoned even as he tried to resist it.

"So you won't push too hard on getting things in order around here? You'll let me settle into this arrangement?"

"Yes, ma'am. But only if you're willing to let me help you get things up to speed—whatever that speed might be."

She got up, brushed off the back of her skirt. "Okay then. Since I'm the boss, I say it's lunchtime. C'mon in and let me feed you for your troubles."

"That sounds good, except…who cooked lunch?"

She slapped him on the shoulder. "It's just sandwiches and chips. Even I can't mess that up."

"That's good to know."

"Now about dinner—"

"Maybe we can grab a bite down at the festival."

"Good idea, since I don't have to provide dinner for our guests." She turned at the door, smiling down at him. "Hurry up. Your sandwich might get stale."

Adam started gathering his tools. "I reckon I am hungry, at that." Putting everything in a neat pile by the back door, he said, "Hey, tomorrow I thought I could cook a roast for Sunday dinner. You know, after church."

Stella whirled just inside the open kitchen door. "Who said anything about church?"

Holding a hammer in his hand, Adam replied, "Well, I just thought…I mean…I plan on finding a church nearby."

"Good for you."

"You won't come with me, and bring the boy?"

She looked down at her turquoise sandals. "I told you, I only get sprinklings of faith from my daddy, and right now that has to be enough. I don't have time for church."

"Oh, I see. Then can Kyle come with me?"

She shook her head. "You're rushing things again, Adam. I don't want him expecting too much, too soon, from someone who's just here for a little while."

With that, she was gone, leaving the scent of something sultry and sweet in her wake. And leaving very little doubt in Adam's mind that he didn't want to get on Stella's bad side. But he sure wouldn't mind getting on her good side. And soon. And it might help both of them if they learned to lean on their own faith, instead of grasping at grains of it from other people.

"I wish Papa had come with us," Kyle said later that afternoon as they strolled down the hill toward the festival on Central Avenue. The Hill Wheatley Park and Plaza was filled with people enjoying the nice spring weather and the rows and rows of all types of arts and crafts. From somewhere inside the park, a jazz ensemble's lively music wafted out over the trees.

Stella glanced down at her son. "Papa's knees are bad, honey. It's hard for him to walk very far."

"He needs new knees," Kyle said, looking up at Adam.

"Yes, he sure does," Stella agreed. "But Papa is fine back at the house. He's taking a nice long nap, and later he's going to set out the cookies and muffins Adam baked yesterday for our guests to snack on when they get ready for bed. So we'll bring him back a grilled chicken sandwich for dinner."

"Okay." Kyle skipped ahead. "Can I have some cotton candy?"

"Maybe after dinner, if you're not too full. And don't run too far ahead. It's crowded."

Stella watched her son, then stole a look over at Adam. He had showered and now wore a fresh black T-shirt and faded jeans, his dark hair spiky and crisp against his olive skin. Stella could smell the clean evergreen from the soap he'd used. Adam cut a striking figure and turned a few female heads, Stella noticed. He turned her head just a tad, too. After all, she was only human. And female. Not dead.

At least, she felt little sparks of life shooting through her with tiny jolts each time she glanced at him. Or each time he looked at her. Telling herself to just ignore all that, Stella tried to focus on some of the paintings displayed along the busy sidewalks.

"Thanks for coming," she told him. "It's hard enough to keep up with Kyle when it's not wall-to-wall people. I appreciate the extra set of eyes."

Adam scanned the crowd, his gaze set and determined, and reminding Stella that he had been a big-city cop. She could almost see that in the way he went on full alert now, scoping the plaza and streets with a keen, but subtle appraisal.

"You don't have to worry much about crime here," she said, hoping he would relax. The man was as intense as a drill sergeant.

"Old habits die hard," he said, shrugging. "A lot can happen in the blink of an eye."

Stella kept her eyes on Kyle, then called to him. "Honey, stay close, okay?"

Kyle came running back. "I'm hungry."

"We'll eat soon enough," Stella replied as they strolled by the Buckstaff Bathhouse. Pointing toward Bathhouse Row, she told Adam, "I could sure use a good hot mineral bath and a massage. One day."

"That sounds nice," Adam said, agreeing. "I've never been one for that kind of luxury, though."

"Oh, me, either. But a lot of people come here to

be pampered. And they say the natural hot spring-water is good for the soul."

"All the more reason to give them a good place to stay."

"You don't let up, do you?"

"Not much."

His look told her he wasn't just talking about remodeling her house. Telling herself to keep her eyes in her head, Stella went over the list of reasons she shouldn't be attracted to this man. He was a stranger; a wanderer fresh off some sort of melt-down, she imagined. He might be in crisis mode. And she'd had enough of crisis mode with her mother and her husband. Now she only wanted a nice quiet life, full of steady, solid work and raising her son. She wanted to take care of her daddy and Kyle. That's all she asked.

And that meant she didn't need to fill her head with images of a dark-haired, hardworking man whose gray eyes spoke of misery and torment. But you can at least be nice to him. The man is trying to help you. And he can cook, remember? Even if you're not sure you can trust his motives.

Stella shifted her gaze back toward Adam. He kept glancing around, taking it all in. The art was colorful, the crafts interesting and eclectic, the music going from jazz to gospel to high-school bands doing their routines. But Adam seemed as tense as ever, almost as if being in this crowd was making him more uptight than relaxed.

"You okay?" she asked, worrying when she had no business worrying.

Adam nodded, kept looking around.

"Nice," he finally said as they came upon some still-life pictures depicting Hot Springs Mountain, while the real thing stood sentinel just behind the park. "It's been a long time since I've seen any hills."

The park was part of the Ouachita Mountain range on the eastern side of the state. Stella looked up at the trees and rocks. "I guess I just take it for granted. But you're right. It is nice, especially with spring bursting out everywhere."

"We can climb to the top if you wanna," Kyle suggested, eager to take off.

"Hold on," Stella said, grabbing her son by the arm. "It'll be dusk soon. No mountain climbing to-night."

"Oh, all right." Kyle twisted. "Then what can we do?"

Adam leaned down. "How 'bout we go in that shop over there and look at the toys. Maybe we can find you a coloring book or a miniature race car for your collection."

"You'd do that for me?"

"Why, sure." Then Adam looked at Stella. "I mean, if it's okay by your mom."

Stella bristled at Adam's ready generosity, but told herself to cut the man some slack. He seemed to need to be generous. He actually seemed to care. Which was refreshing if not disturbing. "I guess one racer wouldn't hurt. Just one more for me to step on, but who's counting?"

"I only need three more," Kyle said, holding up three fingers. "Then I'll have the whole co-wet-sion."

"It's collection," Stella corrected, grinning.

"Well, then, we'd better get started," Adam said, his stern expression breaking into a smile.

Stella had no choice but to hurry and follow her son and the new man in her life across the street.

The new *handyman,* she revised. He's not in my life, he's just here. He just appeared here. Out of the blue, she reminded herself. Like a gift from heaven. Either a gift or a very big mistake. Stella wasn't sure which just yet. But she was sure of one thing. Adam Callahan looked dangerous, and not just because he carried the baggage of a burned-out cop. More like, because he was so good-looking and so intense. Just like her dead husband had once been. Good-looking and intense made for a whole slew of heart-aches. And Stella would not make that mistake again, no matter how impressed she was with Adam Callahan's muffins.

# Chapter Four

Adam couldn't believe how much fun he was having. He actually couldn't remember the last time he'd laughed and smiled so many times in one day. Stella's smile could do that to a man. She wasn't pretty in the cover-girl kind of way. She was exotic and whimsical in her long flowing skirt and pretty lace blouse, with her red-blond hair cascading around her shoulders and down her back like a golden waterfall. That made her much more interesting than any cover model. And she was sure different from all the brash, fast-paced women he'd tried to date back in New Orleans. But this woman's attitude was as fickle as a prevailing wind. Stella fit the stereotype of a provincial country woman, but at times she broke the mold and shattered all his preconceived notions. Which made her so interesting, Adam couldn't resist just being around her.

They'd walked along the streets of the historic district located on Central Avenue. Adam appreciated the towering live oaks and the turn-of-the-century homes and buildings. "This place is pretty," he said as they strolled on past Bathhouse Row. "Even though it's old and historic, there seems to be a good energy going on."

"Hot Springs is a very eclectic place, that's for sure. A mixture of laid-back artists and hardworking everyday people."

They walked in silence for a few minutes. Kyle held his mother's hand and pointed to things that interested him. Finally, they went into a popular diner to order burgers and fries. Adam had a piece of pie, too.

"That hamburger was good," Adam said, just to test her mood after paying the bill and waving bye to the manager. He was fast learning that Stella had many moods. Maybe it was that fiery redhead thing going on. Inside the restaurant, she'd laughed and chatted with the locals, but she'd sure hushed up when they wanted to get more details about her new handyman.

"Yep." She strolled along now, glancing at the art that lined the streets in front of all the quaint shops. "We have a lot of great restaurants here. And there are always some sort of activities going on around the square, too." Then she looked over toward the mountain. "Me, I like staying at home, cooking something simple. I've never been one for crowds."

"I cook a mean burger myself," he said, smiling over at her. "I'll cook us up a batch next weekend maybe."

"Sounds good."

He glanced ahead, keeping a close watch on Kyle. That one was as slippery as a catfish, dipping here and there, running through the crowd. No wonder Stella seemed so tired; she sure had her hands full with the inn to run, her daddy to watch out for and keeping up with an energetic little boy. From everything Adam could see, the inn was a big responsibility. And he wasn't so sure Stella really enjoyed being an innkeeper. She seemed to be more of a solitary person who didn't like a lot of fanfare or attention.

"When did your mom pass?" he asked, curiosity getting the better of him.

She looked over at him, her green eyes going wide. "Why do you want to know?"

Deciding she'd make a mighty fine bad cop during an interrogation session, he shrugged, "Just wondering how long you've had the Sanctuary."

She tossed her long hair over her shoulder. "She died last year. We moved into the inn a few months after that."

"I'm sorry," he said, meaning it. "Were you two close, in spite of her leaving your dad?"

"No."

That one word summed up a whole lot of things in Adam's mind. He remembered Stella saying that her mother had left them when Stella was ten. That had to be hard on a child. No doubt, Stella still held some resentment toward her mother.

She glanced over at him, then let out a sigh. "My daddy and I stayed in Little Rock after she left. We knew she'd moved to Hot Springs, but we didn't know much about the inn. Just that she lived in a big old Victorian house and that she had gained a following with her art. I think the house started out as some sort of artists' community, then turned into a bed-and-breakfast for financial reasons. But she was well on her way to becoming locally renowned when she got sick. At least that's what the locals tell me."

"You said she was an artist, right? What kind of art?"

"Mostly still life and paintings."

He watched as she glanced over the shops and eateries, her face devoid of makeup and emotion. But he could see the burn of a blush brightening up her freckles. Adam was about to ask her another question when Kyle came running back toward them.

"Mamma, I found one of Grandma Estelle's pictures."

Stella stopped in her tracks, her wedge sandals skidding on the sidewalk, her intake of breath quick and unsteady. "What did you say?"

Kyle grabbed her hand. "I found one of Grandma's pictures. You know, the one with the bird sitting by the morning-glory vine. You told me about that one, remember?"

Stella gave Adam a panicked glance. "I don't think—"

"Mama, come and look at it," Kyle said on a whine, practically dragging Stella along. "It's your favorite one, remember?"

Adam had to step aside to keep from stumbling over a couple holding hands, but he managed to keep pace with Stella and Kyle. They rounded the curve leading toward the Arlington Hotel, then Kyle stopped and pointed to a painting sitting on an easel by a doorway.

Adam looked from Stella's frowning face to the painting. Kyle was right. He could make out the signature in the right-hand corner. *Estelle C.* The painting was just as whimsical in its own way as the woman standing beside him. The red bird sat staring at the budding blue morning glory, his eyes bright with anticipation. But the lush, vivid flower had an expectant look on its blossoming face, too.

The title of the painting was *Awakening.* But Adam couldn't be sure if the bird or the flower was the one most surprised.

Stella seemed just about as surprised herself. He watched her green eyes flash fire before they went dark with memories and regret. "I wonder how that wound up here."

"It's sure pretty," he said, sounding dense to his own ears. "Of course, I'm not an art critic."

Stella saw the estimated value written on a card along with the words Not For Sale, then whirled toward him. "It's worth three times what they're asking, but the shopkeeper must be holding out for more."

While Kyle touched the gilt-edged frame, his big eyes opening in wonder, Adam leaned close to Stella. "Don't say that so loud. Someone will talk him into selling it and resell it for a lot more money."

"More power to them then," she said, turning in a whirl of floral skirts and shimmering waves of hair. "Let's go home."

Kyle glanced up at Adam. "I'm not ready to go home yet."

"I'll talk to her," Adam said. "Why don't you run over to that vendor and get yourself an ice-cream cone."

Kyle looked doubtful, but took the money Adam offered.

"Stay where I can see you," Adam cautioned, watching the boy with one eye while he tracked Stella's retreat with the other one.

He caught up with her in two strides. "Hey, Kyle's getting ice cream, so don't go so far just yet. Let him catch up, then we can go home if you're tired."

She stopped, then set her sights on Kyle. "Look at me, just walking away from my own child. What kind of mother am I, anyway?"

"You knew I'd watch after him."

"No, no, I didn't," she retorted. "I need to be more responsible." She shrugged. "It's just that since we've moved here, I can't seem to focus. I fought it tooth and nail. I didn't want to come here, to see where she'd lived and worked. But…my daddy wanted to do this and I wasn't about to let him run that big old house all by himself. I feel as if I'm becoming more and more like my mother each day I'm in that house, though." Her eyes widened, then she put a hand to her mouth. "Never mind. I shouldn't have said that."

Wondering what else she was trying *not* to say, Adam asked, "You want to talk about it?"

"No." She watched Kyle for a minute, then said, "Yes." But when she looked up at Adam, her eyes were as misty as a lake's surface. "Just not today, okay."

Since he wasn't ready to go into detail about his own messed-up life, Adam nodded. "Okay. We'll head home then."

She nodded, then called out to Kyle. Her eyes on her child, she said, "Thanks, Adam."

"For what?"

"For not forcing me to spill my secrets."

"I'm bad about asking questions," he said.

"You're a cop. Comes with the territory."

"But I shouldn't be interrogating you."

She touched a hand to Kyle's head as they started back toward the store with the painting out front. Looking toward the bright painting, she said, "It's complicated. My relationship with my mother…it just wasn't an easy one."

"You can tell me whenever you're ready," he replied, thinking she was like a painting—all pretty on the surface, but hard to understand and read through all the layers of color. Mighty hard to interpret, this one.

She didn't respond. Instead, she turned to stare at the vivid painting. "I wish I could just buy it back, but I don't have the money."

Adam saw the wistful look in her eyes. And he figured she wanted to buy back much more than just a pretty picture.

Stella busied herself with setting out the snacks she always provided for her boarders. People drifted in and out throughout the day, and unlike a regular hotel, the inn only provided breakfast. But fresh-baked cookies and muffins were a tradition at Sanctuary, even if she wasn't necessarily the one doing the baking lately. At least she'd made the coffee and put out the soft drinks, juice and bottled water. The coffee would stay fresh in the thermal carafe and there was plenty of ice in the ice bucket to freshen the other beverages.

Eyeing the chocolate-chip cookies Adam had baked that morning before they'd walked down to the festival, Stella decided she had to try one. She had a sweet tooth, but she tried to stay within reason. Unless of course, she was nervous and tense. And she'd certainly been that for months now. Seeing one of her mother's paintings today hadn't helped. The vivid colors and quirky style of her mother's subjects only reminded Stella of how her mother had shone and dazzled the world. While Stella had waited and longed to hear that smoky voice calling out to her and her alone. She'd often wondered what had happened to that particular painting, since Estelle had assured Stella that it would one day be hers. Apparently, Estelle had forgotten that promise.

Would Stella forever feel as if she were just standing in her intriguing mother's shadow? Stella had always been waiting out of sight for her mother to notice her, waiting in the darkness, to be on hand as needed. But Estelle had never really needed anyone, especially her daughter. And she'd been willing to abandon her only child for that elusive spotlight of art and fame.

Which made Stella's need to keep this place running that much more of a challenge, and that much more of a necessity. Stella needed this old place, because she still needed her brilliant, tormented mother's memory, too.

So she bit into one of the big, crunchy cookies and then closed her eyes in a moment of pure bliss. "It's a regular sin for a man to be able to cook like this," she reasoned out loud, between bites.

"Is it that good?"

She whirled to find Adam smiling over at her from the door leading to the formal dining room. "You shouldn't be lurking about like that," she said, nearly choking. How could she have missed his footsteps clicking across the floor of the parlor?

"And you shouldn't be getting caught with your hand in the cookie jar," he retorted with a grin.

"Hey, it's my cookie jar." Just to prove her point, she shoved the rest of the cookie in her mouth.

"That it is," he said, his smile indulgent. "Need me to do anything else around here before I hit the sack?"

She glanced around at the gleaming butler's pantry where they kept the snacks on a long antique walnut buffet table. Thanks to Adam's help, she now had the kitchen and this little nook in order at last. "No, I think we're good for tonight. What did you have in mind for Sunday breakfast tomorrow?"

He stepped into the long narrow space, his tall

shadow shutting out the setting sun and cutting off Stella's breath before it even left her lungs. The man sure was intimidating in a scary-handsome kind of way.

"I thought I'd do spinach quiche and oatmeal muffins with fresh fruit. The muffins are cooked and frozen. And I've got all the ingredients for the quiche ready to go."

"And the oven?"

"Fixed that late last night."

She slapped at his arm. "You are worth your weight in gold, Callahan."

He grabbed her hand, his eyes going smoky. "And when you smile, you turn all golden. That's worth a week's salary."

Stella grabbed her hand back, then turned to finish up at the buffet. Right now, as the heat of his words hit her square in the face, she felt as if she'd been turned to a bright red.

"I'm sorry," he said, stepping away. "I didn't mean to embarrass you."

She shook her head. "I'm just not used to getting compliments. It's been a while—"

"And I'm kind of rusty in giving them, I reckon," he replied, his voice low and grainy.

She turned to lean back against the buffet. "I guess we've both got a lot to learn. But you *do* work for me. Maybe we should maintain some kind of professional distance, just to keep things from getting messy."

He folded his arms across his broad chest, which only reinforced his admirable biceps—and her need to stick to the rule she'd just created. Wishing she hadn't eaten that cookie so fast, she tried to swallow. But her throat had turned as dry as burned toast.

Adam gave her a direct stare. "So you're telling me that I don't need to be flirting with my pretty boss?"

"Yep, that's what I'm saying. I mean, you just showed up at my door and you do know how to cook and I needed someone to help me get back on track, but it's only been a couple of days. I think we need to keep things casual and balanced. I'd hate to mess up a good working relationship even before it gets going."

"I understand, boss," he said, his expression a mixture of disappointment and anticipation. "And since I like it here and I like this job so far, I agree. I wouldn't want to get fired for being too forward with my employer."

"Good, then we understand each other."

"Completely."

She didn't see that understanding in his eyes, however, and she regretted that she had to be so firm with him. But the man was just as tempting as those wonderful cookies. And she was way too needy right now to think clearly. Best to avoid any kind of tangled, sticky situations. Best to put her loneliness and her fears out of her mind and concentrate on getting this place back up to the standards her mother had once held for the inn. Standards her daughter had obviously never met.

Adam shifted around toward the front of the house. "Guess I'll just go to my room, like a good little boy."

That made her snicker. "That's right. Take a long time-out."

He shook his head, then smiled over his shoulder. "You are one tough taskmaster."

"I know," she said, "but, Adam…?"

He turned, his eyes rich and dark with questions. "Yes, ma'am?"

"I do appreciate all you've done. I think you're going to be a big help to me in saving this place."

"And that's important to you, right?"

She nodded, her gaze touching on the old, eccentric decor and the faded cabbage rose wallpaper. "Yes, it is, for some strange reason."

Lowering his head, he gave her another one of those level, dark-eyed stares. "Then I'm your man."

Before she could form the words to reply to that particular choice of words, he was gone, the echo of his boots hitting against the hardwood floor of the parlor before she heard the sound of a door shutting toward the front of the house.

"You can't be my man," she whispered. "And I need to remember that."

And because that realization made her sad and left her wanting, she grabbed another cookie and headed to her own room. At least she could enjoy his cooking, if nothing else.

# Chapter Five

"I need a favor."

Adam turned, holding on to the ladder, to find Stella standing on the ground below. "What kind of favor?"

She tossed her long ponytail over her shoulder, then crossed her arms. "I've got to take Papa to see the heart doctor this afternoon. It was the only appointment we could get." She let out a long sigh. "He has a bad heart and bad knees. He was in construction for years on end—worked too hard most of the time and now he's paying for it. Do you mind helping out?"

"No, I can watch the inn."

"I need you to watch Kyle, too. Do you mind?"

Adam came down the ladder, then wiped his brow with the sleeve of his T-shirt. "No, I don't mind. Not at all. Me and the boy'll be just fine."

"He's a handful and he'll try to get out of doing his lessons," Stella said, shading her eyes from the bright sun. "He rides home with a friend of mine who lives around the corner. She has a son a couple of years older than Kyle. He'll want a snack, then he knows to do his homework."

"They have homework at his age?"

She laughed. "Just word pictures and learning how to write correctly. And maybe some light reading."

Adam let out a sigh. "Guess I don't know much about kids."

She grinned. "Didn't you say you came from a big family?"

"Yep. Two sisters and a baby brother." He didn't want to go into detail, though.

Stella's laughter rang out over the still backyard. "Two sisters? No wonder you know how to handle women."

He watched as realization caused her freckled skin to turn a pale pink. And he couldn't help but add to her discomfort. "So you think I know how to handle women, huh?"

She looked everywhere but at him. "I didn't mean it exactly in that way, Callahan." She shrugged. "It's just that…well, you've seen me at my very worst—having a hissy fit in the middle of the kitchen—"

"You were having a bad day."

She laughed. "You could say that. But that's the

thing. I don't like having bad days. I'm not one for a lot of feminine theatrics. That was more my mother's way of handling things. You know, high drama on a daily basis."

"I've seen lots of feminine theatrics in my day, that's for sure, so, yeah, I get it. But that doesn't mean you aren't entitled every now and then. And I'm sure not gonna hold it against you."

"That's what I mean. You handled the situation with tact and understanding. I'm not used to tact and understanding."

She looked so uncomfortable, he regretted teasing her. "Hey, it's okay. We all have meltdowns now and then."

"Not me," she said, shaking her head. "I was always the one who had to keep things together, at least when my mother was still around. Then after she left, I had to grow up really fast just to help my daddy. I don't have meltdowns."

He leaned against the ladder, hoping to hear more of the story. "So you took care of things, right?"

She nodded. "Can you see a pattern here? I took care of things whenever my parents would fight. I'd cook and clean, hoping to impress my mother. But she never noticed. Then after she left, I took care of things, trying to help my daddy. He was too brokenhearted to notice." Pushing at her bangs, she looked down at the flower bed. "Then I married Lawrence.

He was too good to be true—literally. So I had to learn how to take care of him, in order to keep him, or so I thought. That is, until I wised up on that account. After I had Kyle, I only wanted to take care of my son and protect him. And now, things are coming full circle. Kyle's daddy left me broken-hearted and with a pile of bills, so Kyle, bless his heart, thinks he has to take care of me. I aim to break that particular pattern." She shrugged. "I just want my son to be a little boy for a while longer."

Adam lifted off the ladder. He wanted to touch her, to push her long bangs away from her face. But he held back. "So what you're telling me is that you're a very good person, but you're tired of being the 'go-to' girl?"

That made her smile, but it looked forced and unsure. "You might say that. Right now, I'm torn in three directions with taking care of my daddy, my son and this place." She held up a hand. "And normally, I'm not one to complain—"

"You need a spiritual advisor," Adam said, trying to help.

"Excuse me?" She looked as if she'd seen something disturbing, the way her eyes went wide with fear.

"Church," Adam replied. "I meant to explain that to you a little better the other day. I'll always be in church on Sunday, after breakfast. I just need that hour or so to regroup. Hope you don't mind."

Stella shifted on her espadrilles, her wide-legged capri pants falling around her calves. "It's not like I'm going to dock your pay, or something. To each his own."

"You don't do church at all?"

She shook her head. "Church hasn't done very much for me. I've learned I can only count on myself."

Surprised at the determination in her eyes, he asked, "So you don't believe in God?"

"Oh, I believe in Him, but I'm not so sure He believes in me. No one else except my daddy ever has."

Adam's heart hurt for the pain he saw in her eyes. This pain went deeper than any hissy fit or meltdown. This seemed to stem from a lifelong acceptance and understanding of hard luck and bad things happening. No wonder her mood changed so quickly from minute to minute. She wasn't centered in Christ.

Adam felt his faith returning twofold as he stood there, wanting Stella to feel the same way. How could he have ever doubted that God had a plan for him, after all?

"Have you ever stopped to think that God does believe in you, Stella? I mean, you have to see the blessings in life to understand that it's not all bad."

She glanced around. "I don't see any blessing here, sorry."

Adam couldn't let that slide. He grabbed her hand. "C'mon."

She balked and pulled away. "I've got laundry to fold. We've got a couple from Dallas checking in today. They want the Morning Glory room and you know that one requires special treatment."

The Morning Glory room was pretty and apparently very special. It was the large turret room at the back of the house on the second floor, complete with a big brass bed and morning-glory-sprinkled wallpaper and white lacy curtains. Stella liked to put fresh flowers in the room to greet the guests, chocolate candy on the pillows and fresh soap and good-smelling linens in the bath, just as they did with every room. But she was especially picky about that room for some strange reason. She fussed with fluffing the pillows and polishing the gleaming oak furniture. And, he remembered, one of her mother's paintings hung over the fireplace in that room. This one was of a surprised morning glory looking down on a white picket fence as if it wanted to escape its boundaries. Adam sure knew that feeling.

"I'll help you get the room ready," he said. "Right now, you need a break."

She gave him a curious, cautious look. "What are you going to show me, Adam?"

"The things you can't see," he replied. He took her hand again, glad she didn't pull away this time.

* * *

Stella couldn't imagine what Adam had in mind, but then she was fast learning that this quiet, unassuming man wasn't all macho flash. He might have been a tough-guy cop back in New Orleans, but she could see that Adam Callahan had a gentle streak a mile long. Hadn't she witnessed that gentleness firsthand with the way he treated her son and her daddy? And *her,* she reminded herself, the warmth of his fingers wrapped against hers as solid as the sun shining down on them. He had always been very gentle with her. Which made him a paradox in Stella's eyes. And made her wonder what it would be like to spend time with such a man.

Bad idea, she reminded herself. Very bad idea. She didn't have time for daydreams or gentleness. She had to keep working, keep going.

And besides, she could see that he was all gung ho about religion. Just another surprising twist to the man who'd showed up at her door looking for a room.

He brought her to a halt in front of the white wooden fence at the back of the property. "Can you see it?" he asked, excitement coloring his eyes.

Stella let out a tolerant sigh. "I see a fence with cracking, peeling paint. I see honeysuckle vines that are probably teeming with spiders and snakes. We probably need to clear out some of those weeds. I see—" She stopped. "What was that noise?"

Adam held a finger to his lips. "Listen," he whispered.

Stella heard it again. A series of tiny chirping sounds. "Are those birds?"

Adam nodded, then pointed to one of the ancient honeysuckle vines. "Look right inside that big branch there."

Stella leaned forward, then put a hand to her mouth. "Baby doves?"

"Sure is," he said, grinning. "I've been watching the mama for days now. She comes and goes. The daddy, too, I think. They've been watching over their little ones. If you listen real early in the morning, you can hear them cooing to each other, calling out."

Stella couldn't stop the tears forming in her eyes. "That's so sweet."

"And that's why I haven't cleared this part of the yard yet," he explained. "I'm giving them time to find their wings."

Stella sniffed, then inhaled a breath of sweet honeysuckle. "That is very considerate of you, but what's this got to do with religion?"

He tugged her away from the bushes. "This isn't about religion, Stella. This is about God. This is about life. You want to protect your little one, same as the doves. God is trying to do the same thing for you."

"Yeah, sure," she said, turning to stomp back toward the house, afraid she'd burst into tears if she actually bought into his way of thinking. "And right now, *I've* got things to take care of. But thanks for the Bible lesson, Callahan."

He caught up with her in the middle of the yard, spinning her around, a look of frustration in his silvery-blue eyes. "You are sure one stubborn woman, do you know that?"

Because she was confused, she mimicked him. "This has nothing to do with stubborn, Adam. This is about having to be responsible, having to keep going. This is about knowing you can only depend on yourself."

His hands on her arms, he asked, "What got you so all-fired cynical and bitter?"

Stella looked up at him, wishing she had his faith and his courage. But she was too tired to even try and find any strength. "Look around," she said. "My father is old and ill. My son is confused and way to smart for his age. He's seen too much in his short life, too much pain and chaos. And me, I've seen the way human beings can hurt each other. I don't see God in that picture. I'm sorry, Adam, but I don't."

"Then you're looking in all the wrong places," he retorted. "You saw that little nest. Those birds don't think about things. They just trust in God. He has His eyes on the sparrow."

"Yeah, well, what if a big old hungry cat comes

along and eats their babies?" It was mean, she knew, but it was also realistic.

"They'll still have each other," he said, his hand stroking her bare arm. "And they'll still have God."

"And that's supposed to bring them comfort? That's supposed to bring me comfort, Adam? I don't think so."

She watched as he hesitated for a few pulse beats, then pulled her close, so that she was forced to look into his eyes. "Listen to me, Stella. I think God puts us in certain places for a reason. And maybe...maybe he put me here in this place to help you."

Confusion and a solid fear rattled her system. "So you rode in on your white horse to rescue the damsel in distress? And throw in a Bible lesson, too? You really are too good to be true, you know that?"

He shook his head, but held her steady. "No, I'm not as good as you seem to think. I walked up, tired and beaten, looking for a room in the inn. And I found you. I'm saying maybe we can help each other. Comfort each other."

Stella saw a raw hope, coupled with a deep need, in his beautiful eyes. But she wasn't ready to fall for a pretty man with pretty words again just yet. "You *are* helping me, Adam. You *work* for me. And we're burning daylight, standing here having a heavy discussion about the true meaning of life. I get it—I need to look at the bright side. Except so far, I haven't seen one."

He pushed away, throwing her a defiant look. "Okay, then. Just be that way. Be all negative and gloomy. But just remember, while you're wallowing in all that self-pity, the world is still spinning away and you just might be missing out on some of the best things in your life."

Stella knew he was right, but she couldn't bring herself to give him the satisfaction of figuring her out in such a short time. "Yeah, well, while you're out there smelling the roses and seeing the beauty of things, stop and remember that life isn't always beautiful, Adam. You of all people should know that. I'm sure you saw some ugly stuff being a cop in a big city."

He came stalking back then, and Stella had to swallow. The man sure looked intimidating when he frowned.

Getting too close, he pointed a finger in her face. "I saw the worst of life down there, especially after the hurricanes. You get it? I saw things no man should ever have to see, but I still believe in the hope of life." Then he pointed toward the back fence. "I believe just as those birds believe. I *know* He has His eye on the sparrow." Then he stood back, letting out a shaking breath. "How else could I survive, Stella? How could any of us survive without the hope of Christ to sustain us? Think about it. You need some hope in your life. That's all I'm saying."

Stella watched, her eyes burning, as he stomped up the porch steps then slammed the back door behind him. She watched and she listened, her mind brimming with a need to call out to him to help her see things his way.

Oh, how she longed for a bit of hope. How she craved a place to just cradle her head, a strong, dependable shoulder to cry on. But she'd been taking care of business for so long now, she didn't know how to let go and rely on anyone else. Especially God. Especially an interesting, enticing man who seemed to be the exact opposite of everything she'd always known. Where was her hope? How had she lost her joy?

Then she heard the faint sound of the baby birds chirping, and she wondered…did God really hear the little birds?

And did God listen to the rants, fears and pleas of a bitter, scared woman who'd lost all hope?

# Chapter Six

Stella came home to find Adam and Kyle sitting at the small dining table in the private apartment across from the kitchen. They were both so intent on Kyle's math work sheet, they barely glanced up when Stella and her daddy entered the room.

Wally glanced over at her, his eyes bright in spite of how tired and drained he looked. Then his gaze touched on his grandson. "That's a nice picture."

Stella clutched the grocery bag in her arms. "Daddy, why don't you go and lie down until dinner. I'll have it ready in a few minutes."

They had not received a good report from the doctor. Basically, her father's weak heart was shot and no amount of surgery would correct that. Between the cholesterol and high blood pressure, her father had to be monitored at all times. And she would be the main one doing that monitoring.

Kyle glanced up. "Mr. Adam's done cooked dinner, Mama."

Stella didn't know whether to shout for joy or sit down and cry. "It's 'Mr. Adam has already cooked dinner,' honey."

Kyle shrugged. "That's what I said."

Wally grinned, then shuffled toward his room. In spite of his jovial nature, Stella could tell he was exhausted. "Call me when it's on the table."

Both Adam and Stella said, "I will." Together.

Stella squirmed for two seconds, then pivoted toward the kitchen. She couldn't be mad at Adam for helping out. It was nice to come home to a cooked dinner. At least tonight would be quiet. The couple coming to stay in the Morning Glory room wouldn't be checking in until well after dinner and they were so regular, they knew where the key was to their suite. An easy night. Especially since she didn't have to cook. Maybe she could catch up on some bill paying and start reading that novel she'd bought at the discount store. Or she might even go out and work on some of her china painting. It had been a long time since Stella had even thought about her own artistic hobby.

The kitchen sure smelled good, she reasoned, her earlier distorted displeasure with Adam's kindness evaporating. She reasoned she was trying to ignore the good in the man for her own safety and protection. She didn't want to get used to depending on Adam Callahan, or any man, ever again. When she heard his footsteps behind her, she whirled and almost collided with him. He took the bag from her and set it on the counter.

"Hello," he said, looking sheepish and unsure since their earlier disagreement.

"Hi," she replied as she busied herself with putting away the milk and butter, the scent of something good tweaking her nose and her curiosity. "What's cooking?"

He gave her a long look that indicated a whole lot more than just whatever was bubbling on the stove. "Spaghetti. Kyle said it's his favorite. That is, after pizza and hamburgers, of course."

That made her smile. "That boy can put away some food. And he does love spaghetti, even if it's just from a jar."

"Uh, I made this sauce from scratch."

"Of course you did," she retorted, her jealousy flaring up with a green-eyed ugliness that instantly made her feel ashamed of herself. Adam was being way too kind and she just wasn't used to that. When had she become so jaded and cynical, anyway? Probably the day she watched her mother pack up and drive away. Or maybe after she'd found out her husband had whittled away most of their savings.

Adam gave her another long look. This one a tad

more chilled than the last one. "You don't like homemade spaghetti?"

"No, I love anything homemade." She stopped stocking the pantry and turned to face him. "It's just that I should be cooking for you. I didn't hire you to come in and take over all the duties."

He frowned down at her. "Is that what you think? That I'm taking over around here? That in spite of what we talked about, I'm steamrollering you?"

She heard the hurt in his words, and wished she didn't have such a snarly mouth. "No, I appreciate you. You know that. But you need time off, too. I mean, you babysat my son all afternoon—"

"It wasn't babysitting. I had fun. Kyle's a special little boy."

She nodded on that account. "True, but he can be tiring, I know. And in the meantime, you managed to whip up a batch of homemade spaghetti sauce, too? See what I mean?"

He leaned his hands down on the counter, then lowered his head to give her a hard stare. "Well, no, Stella, I don't see what you mean. Either I take over some of the cooking duties, or I don't. You tell me."

She slammed canned beans on the counter. "You cook for the guests. That was our agreement. I don't recall ever telling you to cook for us."

"Oh, I get it. You're mad because I cooked something just for you and your family? And that means I'm pushing the envelope, right?"

"I'm not mad, exactly." She looked down at the animal crackers she'd bought for Kyle. "I just seem to be having a hard time accepting your kind deeds. I'm sorry."

Adam leaned close, then whispered. "Why don't you just relax and enjoy having some help for a change? It won't kill you, will it?" Then he managed a smile. "I didn't poison the spaghetti."

"It doesn't smell poisoned," she reasoned, mustering up a little smile of her own. "I'm just tired. It took forever with the doctors, then we had several prescriptions to fill."

His gaze turned soft with understanding. "How's your dad?"

"About the same. His heart is old and ornery. Two surgeries and several medications keep him ticking, but I still can't help but worry about him. His heart is basically shot. We do what we can, but it's not easy." She shrugged. "And that keeps me on edge."

He nodded. "Then I won't be offended by your crankiness. Now, why don't you go rest, too. I'll call you when dinner is ready."

She closed her eyes, weariness seeping through her bones. "I guess I might as well. You seem to have everything under control in the kitchen."

He nodded. Then he said, "Next time, I'll ask first, okay?"

"Okay." She finished putting away the groceries then headed up the hall to her tiny bedroom. "I'll just take about fifteen minutes."

"Take all the time you need. The longer this simmers, the better it'll be in the end."

Stella took that statement to heart. That was exactly what she was so afraid of—if she let this attraction keep on bubbling and simmering, she might not be able to stop her feelings in the end. And she knew there would be an end.

There always was.


Stella woke up with a start, surprised to find it full dark outside. How long had she slept? Glancing at the horse-and-carriage clock on her nightstand, she groaned. She'd been asleep over an hour! Jumping out of bed, she straightened her blouse then went into the bathroom to wash her face and comb her hair. Not one to be lazy, she was appalled that she'd taken a nap when she should have been busy with her daily tasks. She was almost out the door, when she turned and rummaged through her scant supply of makeup to find her lip gloss. Only because she looked so haggard, she told herself.

Or maybe because she wanted to be presentable for Adam Callahan, that voice inside her head responded. Well, couldn't a woman try to make an effort? She'd been so whipped when they'd gotten home, she hadn't even bothered combing her hair. Being exhausted was no excuse for ignoring good grooming, after all.

Her stomach growled with a loud demand as she entered the kitchen. Where was everyone? Then she heard laughter coming from the backyard. Noticing the spaghetti pot still on the stove, she went to the back door and looked out.

Adam, Kyle and her father were all sitting at the picnic table, eating away. "Another nice picture," she whispered, thinking Adam Callahan seemed to fit right in around here. Astonished at how that notion dueled inside her brain between being good and being bad, Stella grabbed a plate and slapped a pile of steaming spaghetti onto it, then grabbed a buttered slice of bread to add to the spaghetti. Finding a glass, she poured iced tea, then kicked open the back door and headed out to join her family.

*My family?*

Her mind was sure playing strange tricks on her with all its wishful thinking. I do have a family, she told herself. I have Daddy and Kyle. And that *is* enough for me. But when she glanced up to find Adam's eyes on her, she thought adding one more to that list might not be such a bad idea.

* * *

He liked the way she moved. Even with a big plate of spaghetti held high in the air in front of her, she was so ethereal, so dainty, that he had to remember to breathe. Stella didn't seem to cater to the whims of the modern woman. She mostly let her hair either hang in loose, curling waves, or she piled it high up in a ponytail. Her clothes looked like consignment-shop castoffs, but they somehow seemed to suit her artsy side. But her eyes, oh, those eyes always looked so direct, so practical that Adam was awestruck with the paradox that she seemed to be. Maybe the free spirit inside of Stella was at war with the responsible woman she presented to the world.

And how could a man reconcile the two? he wondered. Or worse, how could she ever reconcile the two enough inside her own soul to become complete?

"Hey, there," she said, all smiles in spite of those determined eyes. "Did y'all decide to start the party without me?"

Kyle nodded. "Papa said to let you rest."

"That was mighty considerate of Papa," Stella replied as she sank down in one of the old wrought iron chairs across from Adam, her gaze flittering with dragonfly precision right over him. "This sure looks good."

"It's great," Kyle said, tomato sauce all around

his mouth as he slurped up noodles. "Mr. Adam said it's a secret family recipe."

Wally gave Stella a measured look that Adam didn't miss. He reckoned the other two adults at this table might think he was showing off by cooking his mother's famous spaghetti sauce. And maybe he was. But how could he explain that he needed to stay busy and focused, that he was so used to long hours and double-duty stress that just puttering and doing was a joy and a blessing in his life?

Stella took a bite, then closed her eyes. "Mmm, that is pretty tasty. Maybe I can get Mr. Adam to share his recipe one day."

"Can you cook it the same way?" Kyle asked, his eyes going big with disbelief.

"I doubt it," Stella replied, her smile so sweet no one noticed the disdain in her eyes.

No one but Adam, of course. What was he doing wrong here? Should he just back off? He'd have to ask her about that later. Right now, he needed to do some serious damage control. "It's easy," he said to salvage the situation. "Mostly just throw stuff together and let it simmer."

Wally grunted. "Yeah, that makes sense to me."

Adam noticed another meaningful look passing between Stella's father and her son. He didn't know if the two men in her life approved of him or not. Were they trying to make a match, or put out a potential fire?

Stella took a long drink of tea. "It is good, Adam," she said, her smile as soft as the sunset off to the west. And just as full of sizzle. "Thank you for being so thoughtful. I do feel better after my nap."

He took that as a compliment. Then he decided to take matters into his own hands. "Look, y'all, I don't want to overstep my bounds here, so if me cooking dinner upset anyone, I'm sorry, too."

"I'm not upset," Kyle said, tearing into his bread. "But I'm sure gettin' full."

"Then why don't you go wash up and get your jammies on," Stella said, her eyes still on Adam. "Since you did your homework earlier, you can watch a video until I come to tuck you in."

Kyle grinned. "Thanks." Then he turned to Adam. "She doesn't like me watching too much television and stuff. I think that nap did help her."

Wally shook his head as he watched his grandson running toward the house. "That boy is way beyond his years."

"That's what scares me," Stella said, looking down at her food. "He's too smart for his own good."

Her daddy took a swig of tea. "Or he just has a keen sense of intuition. Probably got that from Estelle. That woman could figure things out long before anyone else saw them coming."

Stella stopped eating, then put her fork down on her plate, her whole demeanor changing. She seemed to shrink within herself. "Kyle is not like my mama, not at all."

Then she got up, gathered Kyle's plate on top of the remains of her own food then whirled to head back toward the house, her back ramrod straight.

Wally glanced over at Adam with an apologetic twist to his mouth. "She doesn't like to discuss her mother. And she sure doesn't like me comparing her and Kyle to Estelle." He sighed, then swirled the tea at the bottom of his glass. "I forgave my wife years ago, but Stella, well, she can sure hold a grudge for a very long time."

"I'll have to bear that in mind," Adam replied, still reeling from Stella's quicksilver mood change. Then he looked over at Wally. "And remind me never to cook dinner again without clearing it with her first."

"I'll be glad to," Wally replied. "But we do appreciate it anyway." Wally sopped the last of his bread in the spaghetti sauce on his plate. "Stella is a good woman. She's just used to being in control. Been that way since the day her mama left us. I blame myself for some of her ways. I should have been more of a father to her. But I was young and heartbroken back then. Couldn't see the blessings right there in front of me." He finished his tea, then got up. "Don't judge her too harshly, Adam."

"I'm not judging anyone," Adam replied. "It's not my place to judge."

"Good, then you and me will get along just fine."

Adam knew Wally was being sincere. And he also knew that he'd just been warned to tread lightly around Stella Forsythe. And her father.

## Chapter Seven

Later that night, Adam was back out in the garden enjoying the merging scents of honeysuckle, wisteria and jasmine as he strolled silently around the dark house. Soon the towering magnolia tree out from the carriage drive would be blooming. He could see the iridescent white buds in the moonlight. The smell of flowers made him miss his grandmother's garden back in New Orleans. His whole family had lived on the outskirts of the city and now, most of them were trying to rebuild after the floods and storms. He'd called his mother earlier, just to reassure her that he was doing fine. Of course, everyone wanted to know when he was coming home.

"I'm not sure, Mom," he'd told her "I like it here and I've found a temporary job. Just some handyman work."

"You always did like to putter with wood and paint. Just take care of yourself, son. And remember, we all have storms to get through. Both from the weather and from life. Don't forget that we all love you. And your brother sends his love and, Adam, he's really sorry. You need to forgive him."

"I already have, Mom."

Adam could forgive his brother for getting them both caught up in the bad of this world, but he wouldn't forget what had driven him away from his home. And because he was all alone and nearly broken from all the grief of those storms, he had needed to get away for a while. Maybe that was why he felt so safe and centered here, so far away from the waters surroundings New Orleans. He glanced up at the looming shadow of the mountain that served as a backdrop against the town. That mountain seemed so solid and sure, so formidable. It felt like a great wall of protection around him.

But how long can I just sit here, wishing on a mountain? Maybe his mother was right; maybe he needed to come back home in order to get on with his life.

It occurred to him that Stella and he hadn't really discussed the length of his work here. He couldn't just stay in the Sanctuary House indefinitely, could he? Stella needed to rent that space to make money, not give it over to him for as long as he needed. And while the room and bed were both comfortable, the decor was a touch too feminine and dainty for his liking. But he sure didn't want to leave just yet. There was so much to do around here. Gardening, carpentry, cooking, mending here and there, helping Kyle with his homework, helping Stella get her dad to the doctor. Not to mention getting to know all the interesting guests who came through those doors.

Whoa! Adam stopped his train of thought, halting his restless pacing as he reached the end of the long driveway. All of that sounded kind of long-term and full of commitment. Adam wasn't so sure he was ready for any kind of permanent arrangement.

He shifted back toward the house, hoping sleep would come easy now that he'd had some fresh air. He was stepping up on the side porch underneath the carriage drive when he saw a light click on in the old garage out back. Wondering who could be out there at this time of night, and knowing his cop's instincts wouldn't allow him to just ignore the light, he headed toward the carriage house then peeked through the paned windows.

Stella stood at a worktable staring at a set of old white dishes. Intrigued, Adam watched as she pulled out a carrying case full of paints and started rummaging through them until she seemed satisfied with her choices. He'd heard Wally mention she liked to paint, and he recalled her saying something about that the day they'd met.

Was she about to get serious with some moon-lighting on her hobby?

Not wanting to disturb her, Adam turned to leave but his foot hit an old washtub sitting by the door. The tub rattled and clanged as it skidded on the worn concrete of the tiny patio.

And brought Stella running out the door. "Adam? You scared the living daylights out of me!"

"I'm sorry," he said with a shrug, his hands out in defense. "I saw the light—"

She put her hands on her hips. "Well, what are you doing spying on me like that?"

"I wasn't spying," he said. "I couldn't sleep so I came outside for a walk around the yard. Then I saw the light come on."

She looked embarrassed. "Well, I couldn't sleep, either. So I thought I'd come out here and try to straighten this place."

He glanced around. The studio looked as if it hadn't been used in a while. "Okay. Well, then I guess I'll leave you to it."

She reached out a hand to touch his shirtsleeve. "Wait. That's not exactly the truth."

He turned back, catching her there in the glow of the yellow light. She looked pretty as usual, but tonight her hair was down around her shoulders and back and she wore a loose teal-colored dress that was gathered at the shoulders and smocked across the waist. She looked like something out of a dream. Adam had to swallow hard. "What is the truth then?" he asked, his voice low and grainy.

She looked perplexed and afraid. "I came out here to work. You know, on my things—glazing some of this china, firing up that old kiln, just stuff I've wanted to do. I don't seem to have the time to indulge in this these days."

He smiled at her sweet hesitation. "Why was it so hard to tell me that?"

She tugged him inside the long room. "I feel guilty, dabbling in this when I've got other things to do."

Adam stepped inside the room and took a better look around. "Wow."

Every shelf was covered with her artwork. Stella had painted not only teacups and matching saucers and pots, but she'd also created a few pretty hand-bags and scarves and flowerpots, her whimsical smiling flowers and dainty little figures dancing across the various shapes and designs. An odd-looking oven—or was that her kiln? —sat in one corner, obviously so she could bake the glazes on her ceramic art.

"You did all of this?"

"Here and there," she said with a shy shrug. "Over the years. I brought it all with me when Kyle and I moved." She touched a hand to the china set she had on the table. "My husband didn't like it when I painted. He said I was wasting time, that this was frivolous. Funny, how he managed to do the same thing even when he was supposed to be holding down a job."

"How can this be frivolous?" Adam asked, noting she'd also painted words here and there on some of the objects. Faith, Hope, Love, Peace, Happiness, Patience, Kindness. All of these words shouted at him in pretty pastels and brilliant hues of primary colors. And they told him way more about Stella than she'd ever revealed. "I think it's all real pretty."

"Pretty." She nodded. "Pretty, but what purpose does it serve?"

"Hey, now, don't talk like that. Have you tried selling any of it?"

"A little," she admitted. "When things were so bad for Kyle and me." Her eyes took on a faraway look.

"And how'd you do?"

"I was beginning to make a name for myself, but then Lawrence dicd and my dad got so sick—" She shrugged again. "And after my mother died and I found out I'd inherited this place, well, I kind of gave up on my art. Too much else to do."

"Then you need to get back into it," he encouraged, meaning it. "Stella, you have a talent. I don't know art, but I do know women. My mother and sisters back home would love this stuff."

She smiled at that, lowering her head as she rubbed a finger over a dainty cup. "Most women like pretty things, I reckon. Maybe one day—"

"Why not today?" Adam met her insecure gaze with one of challenge. "Why not now?"

She sighed, picked up a brush. "Because I'm afraid. I'm so afraid things will get out of control, that I'll get so caught up in this I'll neglect Kyle and Daddy."

"You seem like a sensible woman. I don't see you abandoning your family —" He stopped, realization dawning in his dense head at about the time he saw that solid fear cresting in her eyes. "Your mother, right? You're holding back because you don't want to be like your mother?"

Stella dropped her brush and headed for the door. "This was a bad idea."

He snagged her with a hand on her wrist. "Don't think that. Why is doing something you love and you're good at a bad idea?"

She let out a long sigh. "I just feel so scattered, so disoriented. You know, kind of off-kilter. I feel as if I'm trespassing on my mother's memories. Or stomping right across them."

Adam certainly knew that feeling. Holding her hand, he looked down at her long, dainty fingers. "I felt like that after the hurricane hit New Orleans.

My world had shifted and turned upside down. Everything and everybody seemed crazy. I had this big hole inside my soul. I'm not so sure I'll ever fill it again."

She looked at him, understanding in her eyes. "Did you love being a policeman?"

"I did, a lot. I miss it now. But I saw too much pain and suffering. People dying, women being abused, children lost on the streets. It's like that everywhere, but this was my town, my home. I tried to stay. I did stay for these past couple of years after everything started settling down. But it might not ever be the same. And one night, after we got a call for a drug-related shooting, I guess the body count finally got to me. Then, like I said, I had this personal stuff to deal with. I got in trouble with the department, so a week later I resigned, then I left and started driving."

Looking surprised, she shifted her head, her hair falling down around her shoulders. "You mean, you really did just drive until you got to Hot Springs?"

"Yep. Until I saw your sign."

She gave him one of her shy smiles. "Our slightly crocked sign, you mean?"

"It's not crooked anymore. I fixed it."

"So your cooking and mending and fixing, it's not just about needing a job. You needed to keep busy, right?"

"Right." He smiled then, glad she was finally getting it. "I'm not trying to take over your home, Stella. I like working around here. It's nice, calm, peaceful work. And it makes me feel good. You and Kyle and Papa, you make me feel good."

Wrong words. She pulled her hand away from his. "I'd better get back inside."

"What about your work?"

"I can't work tonight. I'll get started soon."

"I interrupted you."

"No, you didn't. I don't think I wanted to paint. I just wanted to visit. Does that make sense?"

He saw the longing in her eyes. "So you're just gonna stand in the shadows, visiting your dreams?"

"For now. Just for a little while."

"I'd hate to think you'll look up one day and see that a little while has turned into a long, long time."

She tossed her hair back, a sure sign that he needed to change the subject. "What kind of dreams do you have?"

Adam didn't know the answer to that question, or maybe he couldn't give her the answer she wanted. Because right now his dreams included watching a pretty redhead paint china. He tried to form the words, then shrugged. "I guess I'm just content to see where life takes me."

"I wish I could let go and be content with that notion."

He tried again. "You can. Come to church with me—just to get a little respite and some peace of mind."

She shook her head. "I don't need to be in a church to converse with God."

"True, but it's a good place to get away from other people's questions and expectations."

"I see it as the other way around. I'd be exposed to people's questions and expectations. I'd have to open up my soul to a roomful of strangers."

"They won't be strangers if you give them a chance. It's more like a sanctuary of sorts."

"I'll keep that in mind."

She whirled like a dancer to leave.

"Hey," he said, wanting to prolong their time together. "I was wondering, just how long did you want me to stick around?"

She seemed confused and put off, her eyes flying wide as she held a hand to the door. "I hadn't thought about it. Something new crops up here on a daily basis, but if you could just finish the repairs and paint touch-ups on the shutters and help some with the gardens and cooking for a while, I'd really appreciate it."

Adam thought about that. He could find any number of tasks to keep him here indefinitely, but that wouldn't be honest or fair. "How about three months? Say around Labor Day?"

"Three months?" She rubbed a hand across her neck. "The end of summer?"

"Yeah. I figure summer's the busy season, right?"

"Spring and summer, but we get a lot of leaf lookers, too."

He laughed at that. "You mean, when the trees change color?"

"Yes. Fall is pretty around here. People love to hike the mountain when the weather gets cooler."

Adam thought about how beautiful the park would be in the fall. He might not be here to see that. "Well, let's shoot for a three-month trial period, okay?"

"Okay."

Did he sense disappointment in her eyes?

Not wanting to push that issue, he forged on. "Anyway, I can't stay in your guest room for three months. You need to rent that to a paying customer. I could move into a hotel or an apartment in town—"

"No." She laughed, pushed at her hair. "I mean, that's silly. I don't mind letting you have the room, but—" She stopped, looking toward the back of the long garage. "Hey, what about the carriage house?"

He glanced around. "We have a carriage house?"

She nodded, pointing toward some stairs tucked away toward the back. "This was it long ago. And there's a tiny apartment right up those stairs. My mama used to rent it out some at first. According to the people who used to work here, she started sleeping out here a lot herself, especially after a long day of painting. And whenever she didn't want to be disturbed." She stood silent for a minute, then said, "You could move in there, fix it up to your liking. Do whatever you need to do."

Adam thought about that. He'd have his own space, but he'd still be on call whenever she needed him. "You don't mind?"

"Of course I don't. It's not much—just two rooms with a tiny efficiency kitchen and a bath, but it's already furnished. Just bring your duffel bag on over tomorrow and settle in." Her gaze hit on the stairs. "I don't go up there much."

"It won't bother you, me living in your mother's private space?"

"It won't bother me at all. I think that room needs a new tenant. And it makes perfect sense, right?"

"I guess it does." Then he raised a hand. "I'll pay rent."

"No, I'm not paying you enough for that, Adam. Just consider it part of your salary. A perk." She grinned at that. "Along with all the other perks—such as babysitting, cooking, taking long walks at night."

He laughed, coming close to stare down at her. "I know one perk I really like."

"Oh, and what's that?"

"My boss," he replied. Then he touched his lips to her forehead in a quick brush. "Thanks, Stella."

Too late, he realized what he'd done. Her startled expression went from confused to vexed in about two seconds flat. "I'm going to… I'm going inside. You can go up and look at the apartment if you want. There are boxes in the back, to pack up any of my mother's things—"

Then she was gone, her skirt swishing through the night as she strutted purposely back toward the big house.

And left Adam purposely wishing he could have kissed her on the lips instead of her cute little forehead.

## Chapter Eight

What had she been thinking that night?

A week later, Stella stood in the kitchen watching the coffee brew, her gaze hovering on the carriage-house apartment. Adam would soon be coming down the outside steps, all full of energy and smiles. How could one man be so happy early in the morning, anyway? And why, oh, why had she offered him the apartment in the first place?

At least he's out of the house, she reminded herself, her hand brushing across her forehead, her memories brushing across that feather of a kiss he'd planted on her that night. Stella closed her eyes, the sound of the coffee gurgling receding into the distance as she remembered his touch, so sweet, so swift. Remembered that and the cloying scent of honeysuckle.

Opening her eyes, she thought about the doves, as she often did these days. She'd see them out in the garden around dusk each night, moving as a pair, strolling together to find worms or seeds. The babies were big now and almost ready to leave the nest. But the doves, they moved together as if they knew eternity would be this peaceful, this content. Why couldn't she have such faith?

This Sunday morning, she knew Adam would walk the short block to the church just up the street. He might even look back toward the house one last time, wondering if she'd ever go on that particular walk with him. And he'd be disappointed to find that Stella wasn't on the path. No, sir. She wasn't ready to take that walk toward getting over her quarrel with God. Not just yet.

And maybe she was fidgety and nervous this morning because her daddy and Kyle had readily agreed to go to church with Adam. Traitors! Then she pushed that thought right out of her head. They weren't turning on her. More like they were turning toward something positive and good. And her son surely deserved to know the word of the Lord. Even if she couldn't quite bring herself to teach it to him.

The coffee belched one last time, causing her to pivot and stare at the offending machine. But the brew smelled good and she had guests waiting in the dining room.

Hurrying around to gather the strawberries and blueberries that would go along with the waffles Adam had promised their current boarders, Stella made sure everything was in order. She'd put freshly cut day lilies on each of the four tables in the big dining room and she'd even brought out some of her own hand-painted china to serve the breakfast of waffles, eggs and bacon. And Adam would help her serve.

By the time she had the coffee poured into the gleaming silver pot, Adam came in the back door, whistling. "Good morning," he said, automatically taking the serving tray. "Ready to get going on breakfast?"

"I was just about to take some of it in," Stella replied, her smile strained. "You can start the waffles."

Since the night she'd offered him the apartment—the same night he'd landed that kiss across her forehead—he'd been as jovial and polite as a politician, all smiles and hard work. Almost too happy. But she'd catch him looking at her at the oddest of times. Sometimes, he'd be perched on a ladder, a paintbrush in his hand, staring down at her as she worked in the garden. Other times, he'd be serving a guest and she'd enter the room, only to have him stop in mid-sentence and give her that long, drawn-out look of his. It was enough to drive a woman into a tizzy.

Pushing such thoughts out of her mind, Stella concentrated on getting her guests served. "Here," she said, pointing to the food tray after he'd finished a batch of golden waffles.

"I got it, boss," he said, a smile in his words.

Adam gathered the long tray that held the eggs and bacon then pushed open the swinging door from the kitchen. Stella listened as he greeted the guests with the same pleasant gusto that he used to greet just about everyone. How could the man stay so positive, when he'd obviously seen the worst life had to offer? Or was that just some kind of front, something he forced on himself to get him over the bad memories? Maybe there was something to be said for being positive. He sure had brightened up this place, in more ways than just painting shutters and clipping hedges.

Maybe he's positive because he also sees the blessings life has to offer.

She didn't like that nagging voice inside her head, but there it was again. Almost as if the Lord Himself were talking directly to her.

Stella offered up plates of food to her visitors, a serene smile on her face, memories of Adam's kiss centered in her mind like the flowers centered on the old, gleaming tables.

"This is mighty good," a tall Texan said, grinning up at her. "I might have to veer off and pass through Hot Springs on my next trip."

"We'd appreciate that," Stella said, meaning it. She was beginning to actually enjoy this. Meeting new people, talking with them about their lives—it wasn't half bad if you had the right attitude.

Adam had the right attitude. He nodded and conversed, oozing charm like syrup dripping from the crystal containers he offered each guest. "Let me know if you want extra blueberries," he told a matronly woman who was wearing a bright pink flower-encrusted hat.

The woman batted her eyelashes. "You are so kind, Adam. And did you say that church is right up the street?"

"Yes, ma'am, Mrs. Creamer. You and Mr. Creamer can walk with me, if you want."

Stella didn't miss his glance toward her, or the wish in his eyes.

"That's a thought," Mr. Creamer said. "At our age, we need an escort."

That brought laughter from the other two couples eating their breakfast.

And so it went. Whenever Adam was in the room, the laughter and conversation just naturally stayed pleasant and happy. So happy.

Aren't you happy? the voice asked.

Stella went back into the kitchen. Was she happy? Would she ever be truly happy? She'd tried with Lawrence, but maybe she hadn't tried hard enough. Lawrence had been sweet and endearing at times, always bringing her back with a smile or a wink and some pretty words and flowers. But mostly, she'd resented his inclination to turn the tables on her and make her feel as if everything bad between them had been her fault. Had it?

Maybe if I'd gone to church back then?

She spooned up strawberries and blueberries, shaking her head. No, not even church would have saved Lawrence from his laziness and irresponsibility. And he surely would have made fun of her if she'd even suggested such a notion.

But Adam thinks going to church might help, she reminded herself. Or rather, that nagging voice reminded her, Adam thinks I need spiritual guidance. Putting both her doubts and the voice in her head out of her mind, Stella rushed back toward the swinging doors.

And right into Adam's arms.

"Sorry." Adam held Stella in his arms, the scent of berries wafting all around them. "I was just—"

"I cut up some more fruit," she said, extracting herself from him, a pretty pink blush covering her freckles. "How's…how are things in the dining room?"

"Everybody's smiling," he said, sensing she needed the space she'd put between them today and over the last few days as much as he did. That kiss hadn't helped things between them, not one little bit. And why was it that he wanted to kiss her on the cheek this time?

"Uh, I came in to get some cream." He held up the tiny silver cream pot. "Mrs. Creamer likes her cream."

Stella started giggling, her hand going to her mouth.

"What?" he said on a whisper, the sound of her laughter intoxicating him. She really should laugh more often. It made her beautiful.

"Mrs. Creamer, cream. Get it. Mrs. Creamer likes her cream."

Adam chuckled, then put a finger to his lips. "She has excellent hearing." He pointed. "Big ears."

"And a big hat."

They both started giggling again, so hard that Adam had to grab hold of Stella to steady her.

Then they stopped giggling. Only to take rushed breaths and stare each other down. Boy, he sure did enjoy looking at Stella. Nice picture, all the way around.

"The cream," he whispered, trying to get back on track.

"The fruit," she answered, looking pretty and flustered.

Adam went one way and she moved at the same time, headed in the opposite direction. They ran right back together trying to get out of each other's way.

Then Stella glanced around to find her studious son staring at them from the doorway across the room.

"Whatcha doing, Mom? Playing tag?"

Adam saw the guilty flush come over her skin as she stammered to answer her son. "Oh, nothing, honey. Just trying to feed everyone. Do you want a waffle?"

"Did Mr. Adam make 'em?"

Stella smiled. "He sure did."

"Yessum, I'll take one. Maybe two. But I have to hurry. Remember I'm going to church with Papa and Mr. Adam."

"I remember," Stella said. She didn't seem as worried about letting the boy go to church as she had yesterday when Adam has first invited Kyle. "You look all cleaned up and ready."

"Papa helped me with my tie."

"That was awfully nice of Papa. Is he dressed?"

"He's working on it," Kyle said as he skipped toward the tiny table where they shared meals. "He said to tell you he's moving kinda slow."

Stella's eyebrows went up. "Is he all right?"

"I'm fine," Wally said as he came into the kitchen. "Just ready for a cup of coffee."

"Don't drink too much," Stella warned. "The doctor said—"

"I know what the doctor said," Wally replied on a grunt. "Now, where's my cup?"

Stella shot Adam a look. "We'd better get back to our guests." Then she glanced toward her father. "It's in the cabinet, Daddy."

Wally held up a hand in thanks, then noisily opened the cabinet.

"Like father, like daughter," Adam whispered before they went marching through the swinging door. "Neither of you is a morning person."

"Nope. We don't talk much in the morning. But I'm learning that I might need to do more of that. The guests seem to enjoy chatting during breakfast."

Adam finishing pouring cream. "Yeah, people like it here for that very reason. It's nice to have people around for the first meal of the day. They don't have to wake up and eat all alone."

Much later, after she'd watch Kyle and her Daddy head off to church with Adam and the Creamers, Stella thought about that. Maybe she and Wally were grumpy in the mornings because both she and her father were always alone first thing in the morning.

But not today, she told herself. Not for the summer at least. This summer she would be able to stand at the kitchen window each morning and wait for Adam to come charging down the apartment stairs and right through the back door, a smile on his face and a song in his heart, bringing sunshine and hope with him. For a little while at least. Adam had brought new life to this old house.

And, she admitted, he was giving *her* a touch of hope. But she wasn't going to get overly confident in that hope. Stella had been disappointed too many times to think things could actually be changing for the better in her life. So she grasped at that hope with a tentative hand, keeping it just out of reach. But she did want to find some sense of purpose again.

With that thought in mind, Stella went out to the garage studio, hoping to dabble in her china painting now that all the guests had left for the day. She needed some time to herself, to think about these new feelings. And with Adam's gentle encouragement, she was eager to get back into her art again. She could do this; she could balance work and play and art and business. She had to do this, for Kyle's sake. True, they didn't have much in the way of money, but if things kept improving around the inn, they just might see a bit of a profit this year.

Maybe it *is* all about attitude, she thought as she strolled out toward the workshop. The house was looking better, but then, so was her attitude. Was that the secret to running a good business? Was that the secret to just getting through life?

She opened the double doors of the old studio,

leaving them open to let the spring air and sunshine flow throughout the long room. The smell of Confederate jasmine drifted in from the bush running along the back fence. The bright yellow-and-white star-shaped blossoms fluttered in the breeze. Deciding she'd try to capture that image in some of her designs, Stella stood just inside the doors, sketching on a small pad. She'd pick a piece of white china, then using a drawing pencil and some graph paper, she'd carefully trace the motif on a plate or a cup, maybe. Then she'd mix the powdered paint on a tile with a palette knife, careful to make sure the paste was smooth and thick. Once she had the colors just right, she'd be ready to paint over the stencil on her porcelain. Stella loved the step-by-step process of readying her supplies for the task. Being alone in the quiet morning, trying to capture the essence of the pretty flowers, did make her feel closer to the Lord.

She heard the doves cooing and wondered why they always sounded so lost and forlorn. But the sound also brought her comfort. It reminded her of Adam.

"Bad idea," she said out loud. She couldn't stand around daydreaming about a man who'd drifted in on the wind. He'd be up and gone soon, and where would that leave her?

"Better, for having known him," she said, a smile tugging at her mouth. With a little gasp, Stella suddenly saw this sweet Sunday morning in a very different light.

"I counted a blessing, Lord," she said, grinning from ear to ear. "Hey, little doves, did you hear that? Stella Forsythe just counted a blessing in her life? How about that?"

Adam Callahan was a walking, talking testament to blessings, that was for sure. But one blessing at a time, Stella told herself. One day at a time.

She still wasn't ready to take that short walk to the church up the street. But she was willing to concede that today, she'd managed to see the world in a very different way. A very positive, contented way.

"Thank you," she said to the heavens.

And then, she heard the doves cooing in unison, as if they, too, were giving their own brand of thanks. That was followed by the chorus of voices down the street at the church, lifting out in a sweet song of praise.

"It's a start."

Stella turned and headed back into her workshop to paint, a smile cresting her face.

## Chapter Nine

Stella finished cleaning her brushes, then checked the plate she'd just painted. Her flowers were vivid and colorful, the creamy white blending nicely with the soft yellows and greens. This was the first application. It was important to layer the colors and go darker with each application so the colors would be rich and distinctive. Satisfied that she'd be able to match the colors to the real flowers just outside her door, she decided to let the plate dry for a few hours then she'd come back another day and deepen the colors until she got it right. After the final drying, she'd fire the teacup and plate in the kiln another time. Feeling good about having this quiet time to create something pretty, she looked around the studio to make sure everything was tidy. Spotting a trunk pushed back under the planked stairs leading to the apartment, Stella wondered where it had come from.

Curious, she went over and tugged the heavy trunk out to open it. Then she saw her mother's initials on it. With a gush of breath, she realized this had probably come from the upstairs apartment. After she'd suggested Adam move in, he'd spent an entire afternoon dusting and sweeping the place. And apparently, he'd cleared out some of her mother's things.

Stella had never gone up into the apartment after her mother's death. And she wasn't so sure she wanted to open this trunk and ruin what had started out to be a good day.

*What are you afraid of?* That voice in her head echoed against the beating of her pulse. Stella knew what she was afraid of. She was worried that if she delved too far into her mother's personal things, she might actually find that side of her mother that remained so elusive and mysterious—that side that had driven her mother to leave a husband who loved her and a daughter who never actually understood her. And if Stella did find something redeemable in her mother's legacy, then she'd be forced to let go of this bitterness that clouded her every waking breath. That same bitterness that had driven her right into the arms of the wrong man. But it was also the bitterness that kept her going, kept her pushing to make something of her life—in spite of not having her mother around for part of her life. If she let all that resentment go, would her life slowly unravel right along with it?

But you have Kyle now. Yes, she had Kyle, her precious little boy. At least she could be thankful for that blessing. Stella couldn't comprehend how a blessing could come from such a bad union. How?

And how could she find any more blessings on this day as she sat here staring at this old, battered trunk? Did she want to open this and ruin her good mood? Or did she want to look for the blessings in the small treasures her mother had tucked away inside this box? Holding a hand to her lips, Stella wondered if true blessings did sometimes appear hidden in the folds of despair. She wasn't ready to test that theory today.

Touching her hand to the aged leather of the old-fashioned trunk, Stella shut her eyes and tried to remember her mother. She saw an ethereal figure standing at an easel. She could remember her mother's tormented eyes staring out into the garden. Estelle would paint frantically at times, as if her life depended on it. Which Stella supposed it did. Then there were the fights—the horrible fights where her father would sit silent and rigid while her mother ranted on and on about how miserable she was, how she needed her art more than she needed the security of a family.

"Well, you got that wish, didn't you?" Stella said out loud, pushing the box back underneath the stairs. She didn't need to open this trunk to find the truth of her mother's desertion. "Another day maybe, but not today."

She refused to get all caught up in her bitterness right now. Instead, she wanted to keep this special Sunday tucked back inside her own memory box, complete with doves cooing and church people singing, complete with sunshine and the smell of paint and turpentine. She'd created something this morning, same as her mother had. But without all the chaos and drama that had surrounded her mother's talent. Her dainty little china plates and cups might not ever fetch a high price in some art gallery, but her china painting meant something to Stella.

It meant she'd turned a corner, that she was willing to risk a part of herself she'd kept hidden away for so many years. She didn't want to mess that up with nasty, bruising memories of being abandoned. Not today.

Getting up, Stella decided to go back to the house and heat up the pot roast she and Adam had let simmer in the slow cooker all night. At least they could sit down and have a nice Sunday dinner. The rest of the day was like a gift; all of the boarders would be gone and they didn't have any check-ins until later in the week. She could paint all day long if she wanted.

She turned to leave the studio and found Adam standing in the door, a look full of curiosity tinged with longing etched on his face as he watched her. And in that minute, Stella could almost understand her mother's intense need to capture images on canvas. Stella wanted to capture Adam, in just this way, standing at her door, waiting and watching.

But she reminded herself as she started walking toward him, how could she capture all the feelings that rushed throughout her system each time the man was anywhere near her? How could she trust those feelings?

Let God paint that picture, the voice inside her head said on a gentle whisper. For once, Stella didn't argue with that voice. Instead, she said a prayer. *I need Your help, Lord.* It had taken a lot to voice that silent little prayer. But Stella had a feeling that prayer was just the beginning of her return into God's loving arms.

Adam couldn't take his eyes off her.

Why did this spry woman seem to have such a firm grip on his battered soul? Why did all of his protective instincts surface each time he looked into Stella's confused eyes? Maybe because Stella was so stubborn, so full of pride, that she just naturally needed a little bit of nurturing? Or maybe because he was the one starving for some affection and nurturing himself? He was glad to see she'd gone back to her painting. Stella's art was different from her mother's. It was more contained and dainty. Her delicate little flower borders and pastel petals falling across plates didn't shout out as much as Estelle's birds and flowers. But then, Stella was not her mother. She fought against any part of being her mother.

"How was church?" she asked as she swept past him, the scent of olive oil and kerosene merging with the sweetness of her shampoo.

"It was nice," he replied, taking in the chaotic tidiness of the studio. He also noted places where he could help improve things—an old shelf replaced here, a table cleared away there. "You should have come with us."

"I had some things to do here." She tugged one of the big doors toward him, waiting for him to move so she could close it.

Adam took the other door and pushed it forward. "What kind of things?"

She inclined her head toward the work table. "I…I painted a plate and a teacup."

He grinned. "That's good. Can I see it?"

"Not yet," she said on a breathless rush. "I have to do a bit more to it, then fire it. Then we'll take a look."

"Okay."

He was pleased that she'd had some time to

spend on her art. Adam knew that had to be important to her, or she wouldn't have set up this studio, here in the place where her mother had also created her paintings. Wanting to express his pleasure, he secured the doors then turned to face her. "I'm glad you had some privacy to paint."

"It was nice," she said, that brief admission spoken so softly Adam almost didn't hear it. "I painted Confederate jasmines on a plate."

Adam glanced over at the jasmine bush. "Good choice."

"I was just dabbling."

"Dabbling is good sometimes. Helps us sort through things."

"Instead of going to church?"

He saw the dare in her green eyes. "You won't get any argument from me, Stella. You know, there are a lot of different ways to feel closer to God."

She cut him a sideways look. "So you're not going to condemn me for skipping church?"

"Not my place to condemn," he replied, hoping this low-key approach would work on her. She was like a little fawn, all fragile and skittish and ready to run at the first sign of trouble, or at the first sign of honesty.

"Thanks," she said as they reached the back porch. "I'm sure hungry."

"Then let's get that pot roast on the table."

Together, they went inside and quietly went about heating up the Sunday meal. Their coordinated movements around the kitchen seemed like a gentle dance to Adam. They were beginning to know each other's habits. He could move around Stella, knowing which way she was headed. He could hand her a bowl and she knew instinctively how to fill that bowl. Adam wondered if she knew instinctively that his feelings for her were changing and growing just like the petunias spilling out from the huge terra-cotta pot near the back door. From the way she looked at him, he thought she knew and felt the same. But Stella wasn't going to be honest about that, not yet at least.

Still, how could he be sure?

Kyle came bursting into the kitchen. "That sure smells good."

"Ready to eat, honey?" Stella asked, her smile bright.

"Yes, ma'am," Kyle replied. "Mama, you should have come to church. The preacher talked all about spring and rebirth and second chances. He said we all get a second chance in life."

"You were listening," Stella said, going about her work. "That's good."

Kyle bobbed his head. "And my Sunday-school teacher, Miss Irene, gave me a picture to paint. Wanna see it?"

"You can show it to me after we eat, all right? We'll hang it right there on the refrigerator."

Kyle bobbed his head again. "I like church."

Adam waited for Stella to give him a look of disapproval, but he was mildly surprised to find her instead smiling down at her son. "I'm glad you like church, honey." Then she looked up at Adam and her smile broadened. "It's been a good day so far."

"Yes, it has," he said, relieved that she wasn't angry with him for taking her son to church. And just because he was feeling bold, he leaned close. "The preacher said there's a gospel and bluegrass band playing on the square tonight. Wanna walk up there later and give a listen?"

"Just you and me?" she asked, her voice grainy with doubt, her eyes wide with surprise.

He smiled. "Uh, yes, just you and me. That is, if that's allowed?"

She pursed her lips and glanced toward her son. "That might be allowed. Let me think about it."

"Okay," he replied as he poured tea. "It starts at six. Meet me in the backyard if you want to go."

She nodded, then scooted away toward the den where her father sat reading a magazine. "Daddy, dinner is ready."

Adam stood at the counter, wondering if she'd show up. And wondering if he'd been wise to ask Stella out on an official date.

\* \* \*

At five o'clock, Stella knocked on the door of the small office where her father sat poring over the inn's accounting books. "What're you doing, Daddy?"

Wally glanced up, a guilty look on his aged face. "Just going over the figures. I thought you were resting."

"I did rest while I folded linens, and then I checked our bookings a second time and then, well, never mind. Why are you going over the books? You know I handle all of that."

Wally put down his pen. "Yep, and that's why I'm going over things. I want to contribute, Stella. I can do this part for you, at least. I kept my own books for years, you know."

She sank down in a chair across from him. "You don't need to do that now, Daddy. It's not that much to do, mostly just putting numbers into the computer."

Wally stared over at her, his bifocals perched on his ruddy nose. "But it's just one more thing for you to worry about. You know, I'm old, but I'm still useful. I even know a little bit about this fancy computer program you had installed. If you give me a chance, I think I can take over the bookkeeping around here."

"But why?" Stella asked, shocked that her father was even expressing an interest in this. "You need to rest and take it easy, remember?"

Wally slammed his fist against the aged walnut

desk. "Yeah, I remember since everybody and his brother around here tells me that on a regular basis. Stella, you work too hard and you have always taken on way too much, sugar. I'm telling you I want to contribute." He stopped, took a breath. "I *need* to contribute, understand?"

Stella heard the catch of frustration in his words. "I'm sorry, Daddy. You did run your own business for years. I guess you might be an asset around here if I'd just give you a chance, huh?"

"Exactly," Wally said, pointing a finger toward the ledger. "I might not know about cooking pretty meals or taking care of frilly sleeping rooms, but I do know figures. And I can do this for you, Stella. I just want to do something productive."

"Okay, then." She got up and came to lean over her father, giving him a hug. "Thanks for offering. When can you start?"

"I already have," Wally said on a grin. "You keep meticulous records, girl."

"I learned from the best," she replied, happy that her stoic, quiet father had confessed his need to feel useful. "And I'm sorry I didn't think of this months ago."

"Well, we've got it all cleared up now," Wally replied, his fingers tapping on the desk, a relieved look on his face. "Now, why don't you go on back and rest some more."

Stella thought about Adam's invitation. "Actually, I might walk into town with Adam. He told me about a gospel group that's gonna play on the square tonight."

Wally shot her a curious look. "Oh, yeah?"

"Would you mind?" she asked, wondering if her father would disapprove. "It would mean you'd be babysitting Kyle for a couple of hours."

But Wally surprised her yet again. "Don't mind one bit. Me and the young'un will be just fine. I can let him beat me at checkers again."

Stella leaned over to kiss her father's forehead. "Thanks, Daddy. We won't be late."

"Take your time," Wally said with a wave of his hand. "I know you'll be safe with Adam."

Stella knew she'd be safe, too. At least, she knew Adam would take care of her. But she had to wonder how safe her heart would be. If she accepted his invitation, she'd be taking a step toward building a relationship with him. And where would that relationship lead?

You won't know until you find out.

In spite of her misgivings, Stella wanted to find out. She wanted to get to know Adam better. And she prayed that God would grant her this one request and show her the way to handle her feelings.

Two prayers in one day, she thought, her mind

reeling with all kinds of new sensations. It felt odd, but good, to lean on a higher source for a change.

After freshening up, she kissed Kyle, admired his picture of Jesus and a little lamb, then headed out into the backyard. Adam was standing by the honeysuckle bush, waiting for her. He turned at the sound of the back door slamming.

"So you decided to come?"

She nodded, her head down as she walked toward him. "Yes. It sounded like fun."

He smiled over at her. "I'm glad you're coming with me. I've heard good things from everybody at church about this group."

Stella didn't think she'd be able to concentrate on the music tonight. She would be too busy trying to ignore her growing attraction to Adam. She needed to remind herself to keep things in perspective.

"This doesn't mean anything, okay?"

He gave her a look that indicated he understood. "It only means that we're going to walk down to the square to listen to some music."

"Right."

He took her hand, then led her through the back gate. Then he stopped, turning her back toward the yard. "Look."

Stella followed his gaze to where the doves were walking side by side, eating seeds and worms, underneath the ancient magnolia tree.

"What a pretty sight," he said.

She nodded, then turned back toward Adam. "Our doves are very loyal to each other."

He smiled. "I wish people could be that way."

Then it occurred to Stella that maybe she wasn't the only one who'd been abandoned and hurt. Maybe it was time she found out what had driven Adam away from his home. And how he'd managed to keep his faith throughout it all.

# *Chapter Ten*

The band's rendition of "Rock of Ages" echoed out over the town. Stella had to admit, the music was soothing and toe-tapping. The tone was a bit country, but with a definite old-fashioned gospel appeal. She hadn't heard these kinds of songs since her early days at vacation Bible school back in Little Rock. But that was before things had fallen apart between her parents, before her mother had denounced organized religion and her marriage vows and had left for good.

No wonder Stella had buried all of those memories. It hurt to think her own failed marriage had somehow mirrored her parent's union. And no wonder she was afraid to even dream of a happy future with another man.

"Hey, you want something to drink? A funnel cake, maybe?"

The hopeful look plastered on Adam's face made her smile in spite of her dark musings. Tilting her head, she asked, "Do *you* want a funnel cake?"

He patted his stomach. "I could eat one, yeah. But I'm willing to share."

She laughed out loud. Adam had Kyle beat on always being hungry. "Okay, one funnel cake and two lemonades. How's that?"

"That I can handle," he said, walking backward as he grinned at her. "Find us a bench. I'll be right there."

Stella nodded, then searched for a place to sit. People had brought their chairs and blankets and were clustered here and there in the center of the park, with the ever-present mountain looming as a picturesque backdrop of rock and trees. She saw a secluded bench near one of the bathhouses, and headed that way. Settling her long baby blue broomstick skirt around her legs, Stella took a breath and inhaled the sweet cinnamon smell of funnel cakes mixed with the more lemony scents of magnolias and fresh grass. Off behind her, she could hear the steady flow of the warm, therapeutic waters that came directly from the hot springs underneath the mountain, bubbling and steaming in a small pool behind the row of famous bathhouses. It was a perfect late-spring day filled with the sounds of gentle music and refreshing laughter. She waved to people she knew and smiled at the many tourists strolling up and down Central Avenue toward the famous Arlington Hotel. The grand old building stood across from the square, where the street split with one road going toward the park and the other continuing through town.

This really was a pretty little town, she thought, wondering why she'd never stopped to enjoy the beauty of her surroundings. Then part of a Bible verse flashed through her mind. *Things hoped for; things not seen.* Stella couldn't recall the entire verse, but she did remember her mother reading that to her once, long ago in their happier days. Maybe that truly was what faith was all about. You saw the blessings in your everyday life and surroundings, but you also accepted the unseen blessings of God's hand on everything in life.

*I might need to take that into consideration, right, Lord?*

She closed her eyes, allowing the warmth of the waning sun to fall across her face, her heart reaching toward that warmth like a flower waiting to blossom. *Help me to see the unseen. Help me to find my blessings.*

When she opened her eyes, Adam was standing a few feet away, a funnel cake on a paper plate balanced in one hand and two plastic cups of lemonade gathered close to his midsection in the other. Seeing the tender expression there on his face, Stella got up to help him with the drinks. And felt her own blush all the way down her neck.

"Thanks," he said, allowing her to take the drinks. "I got extra cinnamon on the funnel cake. Is that all right?"

"That's just fine," Stella said, avoiding the intensity of his eyes as she sat back down. Waiting for him to get the funnel cake centered on his lap, she took the paper napkin he handed her.

"You get the first bite," he said, offering her the flat brown swirls of dough that had been deep-fried to a curling perfection. "I got extra powdered sugar on top, too."

"You sure like a lot of extra trimmings, don't you, Callahan?"

He grinned, then watched as Stella broke off a swirl of the crisp doughnutlike confection. She took a bite, closed her eyes, then let out a sigh of contentment. "That is sure good."

Adam pulled a piece of crusty dough off the paper plate, then bit into it. "Hmm. That is mighty tasty. Why *are* these things so good?"

Stella took another chunk from the funnel cake. "Maybe because they're loaded with all the bad stuff—sugar, flour, grease—the works. But I can't resist them." She took a long sip of her lemonade.

"And they seem to just go with lemonade, don't you think?"

When he didn't speak, she glanced over at him. And stopped chewing. "Adam?"

He was staring at her, his blue-gray eyes going as dark as the deepest waters steaming up from underneath the mountain. "I think…" He stopped, swigged his own drink. "I think…" He reached a hand across the space between them, touching on her lips. "You have powdered sugar, right there."

Stella inhaled at the soft gentleness of his finger brushing across her skin. Little flutters of awareness floated throughout her system much in the same way the powdered sugar seem to flutter up and away from the funnel cake. "Thanks," she said in a hollow voice. Then she caught his finger with her hand. "I'll get the rest."

"Okay." He looked away, back toward the crowd and the music.

They sat silent for a while, each munching on the disappearing funnel cake. Stella wondered if she'd done something wrong. He seemed embarrassed, too. She knew why *she'd* gotten all flustered. She'd wanted to kiss the man, right here in the middle of the park. Not wise. Hot Springs—the downtown artist community of Hot Springs—was a small tight-knit group. Rumors would run amok.

But what was so wrong with her dating again?

She was a good mother and a hard worker. It wasn't as if she were doing something forbidden or wrong, wanting to have a man in her life, was it?

Finally, unable to stand the silence, she dusted off her fingers and turned to Adam. "Are you all right?"

He polished off the few crumbs left on the plate, then tossed it into a nearby trash container. He sank back down on the bench and turned to stare at her. "No, I'm not all right. I have a big problem, Stella."

"What is it?" She worried that he was going to up and quit on her, leave her in the lurch before he'd finished all that he'd promised. "You got something on your mind, Callahan?"

He nodded. "Yeah. *You.* I got you on my mind, Stella. Day and night." He held up a hand. "And I know we had a deal, an agreement that you're the boss and I'm just here for the summer. But I don't know if I can stay that long."

Her stomach went cold, making her wish she hadn't eaten so much of that sugary cake. "Why can't you?"

He turned to her, grabbing one of her hands in his. "Because I want to kiss you. That's why."

Stella held on to his hand, her heart hitting with paint splatter precision inside her chest. "So that means you have to leave? You'd just up and leave because of how you feel about me?"

"I don't have much of a choice, do I?" He shook

his head. "I like it here, Stella, and the Good Lord knows I needed this respite, but I don't want to mess things up between us. I want to finish what I started, but I think something else is starting between us. And I'm afraid you'll fire me if I cross that line."

Stella shut her eyes, said another silent prayer, then wondered if she'd regret her next words. "What if I told you it's okay to cross that line? What if I said...I'd like to kiss you, too?"

Adam swallowed another gulp of lemonade. "Do you mean that?"

"I wouldn't have said it if I wasn't thinking it."

He knew her well enough to understand that. Stella didn't mince words. "What are we gonna do?"

She gave him such a sweet smile, he couldn't look away. "Stella?"

Her smile broadened. "Cool it, Callahan. Don't get into such an all-fired panic. It's been a long time since a good-looking man has looked at me the way you're looking at me right now, so I just want to savor the moment, okay?"

He bobbed his head. "I could look all day and never get my fill of you. But what about that kiss?"

She wiped her hands on her napkin, her smile indulgent and teasing. "We've got all summer, right?"

Adam lowered his head, then ran a hand over his

hair. "Are you trying to drive me crazy here, Stella? 'Cause if you are, it's working."

Her tiny hand on his arm only added to his woes. "Adam, I'm just saying, well, the first time I fell in love it was this big fast rush. It was too rushed, you know? I didn't feel worthy of anyone's love, so I took what came my way and didn't look back. I made a big mistake with Lawrence, but Kyle is the blessing I gained from that mistake. I don't want to make another mistake."

"You think kissing me would be a mistake, then?"

"No, I think kissing you would be very nice and pleasant and…good. But I want to take it slow this time. I want to know everything there is to know about Adam Callahan. And all I know right now is that I like you, I think you're a good man and you cook the best blueberry pancakes I've ever tasted."

He gave her one of his own teasing smiles. "Isn't that enough?"

"It could be, if I was the same old Stella. But I've changed. I had to change for Kyle's sake. I won't put that little boy through any more heartache."

Adam saw the doubt in her eyes. And the fear. "I'd never hurt Kyle or you."

"No, you probably wouldn't set out to hurt us, but that's why I'm asking you to take things slow. What if come summer's end, you decide you're ready to go back down to New Orleans? What if you get tired of being a bed-and-breakfast maintenance man in this sleepy little town? Then what, Adam?"

Adam's frustration slid to the pit of his stomach and lodged right there with his indigestion. "I doubt I'll ever go back to New Orleans to stay. I might visit my family, but I don't think I can ever live there again. Too much water under the bridge, both literally and inside my soul."

Stella took his hand in hers. "Okay, but I need to understand why you can't go back. I need to know that about you, too, so I can understand you. Lawrence kept a lot of things from me—nasty, dark things. He wasn't a good man. But you are a good man—a good man who's seen bad stuff. I need to know about it, Adam. All of it. I just want to know, to understand how you can survive something like a hurricane and all that comes with it and still have such a strong faith." Then she gave him a hard stare, pinning him with her green eyes. "Or is this about more than just a storm?"

Adam got up to pace in front of the bench. "I don't know if I'm ready—"

"Exactly," she said. "And I want you to be ready. Because if you can't share your past with me, how can I even think about what the future might hold? You talk about having spiritual guidance, but I need the truth. I've always needed the truth. That's what guides me."

He turned, trying to control the sense of help-lessness cresting like a hot wave inside his system. His faith was strong, but it was also very private at times. It was one thing to invite her to church, but could he let her inside the deepest part of his soul? He wanted to share his beliefs and his regrets with Stella, but he sure didn't want to bare his soul or go back over the horrors of a city de-stroyed. And his way of life destroyed. So he tried to waylay her.

"Is this about your mother?"

Stella got up, the pink of her skin showing that she was wrestling with this, too. "Probably. I never could get the truth out of her. I never could get the truth out of Lawrence. They both died with their secrets intact. And I'm all about the truth, Adam. I'm just too practical and pragmatic to go on any-thing else." She touched a hand to his arm. "I care about you too much to let anything stand between what might be between us. But I need proof and I need answers. I have to know I'm doing the right thing, opening myself up to that kind of hope again. I want you to understand that."

But he didn't understand. He didn't understand how his past as a police officer could possibly have anything to do with the simple, peaceful life he'd found here at the base of this mountain. In his heart, he knew she was right. It had everything to do with his future, and he couldn't deny that. But he tried. "Do you think I'm hiding something, Stella? Is that what this is all about?"

"Yes, I do," she said, her gaze holding his. "I think you're hiding a world of hurt. And I just don't know if I'm strong enough to carry you through that hurt, Adam."

"I don't expect you to carry my burdens," he said, his words harsh. "I've always handled problems myself. I've always taken care of things—" He stopped, remembering how he'd taken care of things for his family. And look where that had gotten him.

Stella gave him a compassionate look that almost broke him. "Maybe it's time you listen to your own advice, then. Maybe it's time to let someone else in on *your* pain and suffering."

Adam didn't get this woman. "But you just said you weren't sure if you wanted that job."

"No, I said I don't know if I'm strong enough to help you—unless you open up to me now." She shrugged. "I guess I don't like surprises and drama. My mama left all of a sudden, without explanation. If I'd known some of what she surely was feeling, maybe I could have helped her. Same with Lawrence. He didn't tell me anything, but I think deep inside that man was suffering more than I ever realized. He didn't let me *know* him, Adam. I want to *know* you. I don't want you to be a stranger to me the way my mother and my husband both were. I care about you, so it has to be right."

Adam digested that, thinking at least she did want *something* from him. But he couldn't bring himself to just sit down and pour out his heart to her. His feelings were still too raw, too muddled and confusing. And besides, she might think the worst of him for what he'd done. "I need time, Stella."

She stared across at him, her green eyes misty. "We both do. That's why we need to go slow and get to know each other."

They stood there, a few inches separating them as the sun begin to set off to the west, the sound of "Precious Memories" drifting out over the still air.

Adam reached out toward her, then dropped his hand. "So what do we do now?"

"We walk home," she replied, taking his hand.

Adam fell in step with her, the warmth of her slender fingers touching him like threads of light. "I guess I don't get to kiss you yet, right?"

She slanted him one of her famous Stella looks. "Not just yet. But you can keep right on thinking about kissing me. I don't mind that one bit. And if you throw in a funnel cake now and then, we just might make it, Callahan."

Adam knew he wouldn't have a problem thinking about her. Not at all. The problem would be in trying to figure out how to win over this stubborn, pretty woman somehow.

Without having to open a vein to do it.

## Chapter Eleven

Stella listened at the open kitchen window, a smile on her face in spite of how tired she was this morning. Adam and Mrs. Creamer were out in the garden discussing gardenias. And although Stella hadn't slept well after the heart-to-heart she and Adam had at the gospel music concert, she wasn't mad at the man. Not at all. Adam's presence here had actually caused a kind of awakening in Stella. She had more patience these days, more kindness toward the strangers who showed up at her door. She was becoming more of a people person, and all because of Adam's example.

Score one for the good guy.

Which was why she was standing here, watching him, and getting such a kick out of listening to him talk to the opinionated but ladylike Carlita Creamer.

"It's the best scent in the world," Mrs. Creamer said, sniffing at the big gardenia bush out by the old stone patio just beyond the carriage drive. The leafy bush was bursting with fat, lush white blossoms that reminded Stella of tufts of tissue. "That's why I love the South—so many beautiful scented flowers and trees."

Adam nodded, ever solicitous and courteous. He had such a rapport with the guests. "Yes, ma'am. My mama back in New Orleans has a whole hedge of gardenias. I used to lie awake late at night growing up, that sweet smell drifting in through my window."

Stella stopped washing dishes so she could hear more. If she had to resort to eavesdropping in order to get to know Adam a little better, then so be it. The man might be able to charm the guests, but he was tight-lipped when it came to talking about his past. At least he was with her. But maybe after last night—

"Tell me about your family, Adam," Mrs. Creamer said, her short red hair shimmering in the morning sunlight.

"Well, ma'am—"

"Call me Carlita, please."

"Well, Ms. Carlita—" Stella heard the smile in his respect "—my mother is a good woman. She taught school for years but now she's retired. She works part-time at the public library, but she mostly likes to babysit my nieces and nephews. She and my dad live near a bayou. They got some water damage and had some structural repairs after the hurricane, but they're getting back on their feet. They're always having grandchildren over to spend the weekend. They go boat riding and fishing, hang out on the pier."

"Oh, how many grandchildren do your parents have?"

"Five so far. My sisters each have two girls and my brother has a baby boy. It's like a row of little stepping stones."

There was a moment of silence, then Mrs. Creamer said, "Why do you look so sad? Do you miss them?"

She heard Adam clearing his throat. "I do. But… my brother and I had a falling-out just before I left. I didn't even get to see his new baby boy."

This was news. Stella swallowed back her disappointment. Why hadn't Adam given her this kind of general information. Did he prefer sharing family tidbits with someone who was almost a stranger? Stella stared down at her dishrag. Maybe this falling-out with his brother had something to do with his reluctance to talk about his past. And maybe Stella could ask him about it later, when the time was right.

"My, my, that's a shame. I sure hope you two patch things up one day."

"I don't know. My mama is sure hoping that same thing."

"And what about you, Adam? Do you want to make peace with your brother?"

"I'd like that. If he can ever forgive me."

Something pierced Stella's soul with understanding. So Adam needed forgiveness? Was that why he didn't want to tell her the whole story? Was he ashamed? Stella could understand that concept. She closed her eyes and wished she could help him. And she decided it might not be wise to question him about this.

Mrs. Creamer flittered on with her own questions. "What about you, Adam? Why aren't you married with children yet?"

Stella strained to see his face, but he had his back turned, his head down. He stood in that way she'd come to know and understand, with his hands on his hips and his legs braced apart, his feet solid against the earth.

"I've, uh, I'm afraid I just haven't gotten around to all that yet."

"I can see that. But have you ever considered marrying and settling down to raise children of your own?"

Adam glanced toward the house. Stella jumped back from the window, but kept her ear close, holding her breath as she waited to hear the answer to that question herself.

She heard his sigh on the wind. "I've thought

about it, a lot. But you know, being a police officer doesn't lend itself to a good home life. It's hard, dangerous work. I've dated women here and there, but nothing serious enough to make that kind of commitment."

Mrs. Creamer wasn't buying any of that. "Oh, fiddle. I've known a lot of happily married officers of the law. So stop using that as an excuse."

Stella peeked back out the window, her heartbeat causing the ruffles of her apron to flutter.

Adam lowered his head again, his hand touching on one of the gardenia bushes. "It's not so much an excuse as just a fact of life. My mama says I just haven't found the right woman."

Mrs. Creamer laughed out loud. "Your mama is probably right. But what's your excuse now? You left police work, right?"

"I did. I guess I reached the end of my rope. I was just standing there on the street one day, looking at a homicide victim and suddenly I just couldn't take it anymore. I had a bad experience with some other things, so I decided it was time to leave."

Mrs. Creamer plucked a fat white blossom and tucked it over her ear. "Maybe you're just reaching for another kind of rope—a new lifeline in a new place, away from that harsh life you had down in New Orleans." She waved a hand in the air. "You've got to admit, what you do here is completely at odds with the demanding life of a policeman."

"It is that," Adam agreed, once again glancing back toward the house. Then he lowered his voice, forcing Stella to step close to the window again. "I don't know why I wound up here. I just know I like what I'm doing right now. I like helping out around here. I like meeting nice, decent people. I enjoy helping our visitors to relax and find some sort of rest and solace."

"And in the meantime, you're resting and regrouping, too, right?"

Stella watched as he bobbed his head. "Right. Exactly. But what if I decide I'm rested enough? What if I decide I need to go home?"

Mrs. Creamer took the clippers from him, then cut a few more blossoms. "Oh, Adam, I think you are home. You just don't know it yet." Then she handed him the blossoms. "Why don't you take these inside to Stella."

Adam took the flowers. "She might not—"

"Don't give me any excuses, son. She's listening to everything we're saying." Then she turned toward the house. "Isn't that right, Stella?"

Mortified, Stella backed away from the window without responding. Busying herself with finishing up the morning chores, she tried to ignore the gentle slamming of the back door. Then she smelled the gardenias.

"Uh, these are for you," Adam said, shoving them at her.

Stella turned as he crushed the four delicate white flowers into her hands, her guilt causing her to appear humble and sheepish. "Thank you very much."

He didn't look happy. "You don't have to spy on me, Stella."

"I wasn't spying." She whirled to find a vase for the gardenias. "I can't help it if I happened to be standing at the window."

"Yes, standing and spying," he said as he yanked open the refrigerator and grabbed a bottle of water. "Well, did you get enough information? Are you happy with what you heard me telling Mrs. Creamer?"

"It's Carlita," she retorted. "She asked you to call her Carlita."

"So you were listening!"

"Of course I was listening, Adam. I'm curious about you. Mrs.— Carlita asked some very important questions."

"And I suppose those are the same sort of questions you have, right?"

"I guess so," she said, shrugging. "Women like to know what they're getting into, whether it's hiring a maintenance man or trying to decide about other things."

"Women can drive a man crazy," he replied. "Probably why I never got married."

So much for their delicate coming-to-terms talk last night. And the hope she'd held to her heart since then.

"Is that how you feel, then? You think I'm trying to drive you crazy, just because I want you to open up to me?"

"I don't know. You're asking for things I can't give you right now. Maybe never."

Hurt, she looked away. "Don't worry, Adam. I won't ask you any more questions. Whatever happened down there is your business. But it's clear you can talk to anyone around here about it, except me. I heard that much from your conversation, at least."

He stepped close. "Look, I'm sorry. It's just hard to explain, okay?"

She pulled out a loaf of stale bread to make a breakfast casserole for tomorrow morning. "Okay, but I don't think it's asking so much to get to know you better. I learned more about you in that short conversation than you've told me in three weeks. And I won't apologize for listening out my own kitchen window."

"And I won't apologize for not spilling my guts," he retorted before he downed the rest of his water. "Now I'm going into town to get some plumbing parts for one of the upstairs bathrooms. Want to follow me to the hardware store to see what I say to the clerk in there?"

"I have things to do," she said, wishing he wouldn't stare at her like a whipped pup. "And I'm sorry about being so nosy. It won't happen again."

"I doubt that," he said. "But from now on, I'll just make sure I know where you are before I get into any kind of conversations with our guests."

"Fine, be that way then."

"Fine, I will."

He stomped off, the sound of his boots clicking on the hardwood floor.

Wally came ambling into the kitchen, shaking his head. "Why don't you two just quit bickering and get on with things, Stella?"

"What things, Daddy? What are you talking about?"

Wally shook his head again. "The thing that's eating away at you and Adam," he said. "The thing that Mrs. Creamer and everyone else who comes passing through here can see clear as day."

"Oh, and what might that thing be?" Stella asked, completely flustered now. Did everyone around here listen in on everyone else's conversations?

"You two are falling for each other," her daddy responded. "In a really big way."

Stella cackled with nervous laughter. "Daddy, how can you even think such a thing? We are not falling for each other. It's just that working together day in and day out makes you want to get to know another person. It's all about trust and understanding and feeling comfortable with your coworkers."

"Uh-huh. If you say so."

Stella slammed the silverware drawer shut. "Well, I do say so. I'm not ready to get involved with the first single man to darken my doors. Not ready for that at all."

"Sure, honey. Of course not. I'm just saying—"

"I know what you're saying and I'm telling you that this so-called thing between Adam Callahan and me is nothing to worry about. Nothing at all."

"Okay," Wally said over his shoulder as he hurried back to his accounting chores. "Whatever you say, suga'."

Stella turned back to the window to find Adam standing there staring up at her. "Well, well, look who's spying now," she said with a snap in her voice.

"I forgot my wallet," he replied. "I was coming back to get it and—"

"And you heard everything I just said to my daddy, right?"

"I sure did," he replied, not moving. He just stood there looking up at her with those big, dark blue eyes. "And I sure am glad you cleared all of this up." Then he shook his head. "And after all that pretty talk last night."

Stella felt all hot and red-faced. Maybe she needed to shut this window and turn on the air-conditioning. "I shouldn't have said those things yesterday. We can't have everyone assuming we're an item, Adam. It doesn't do for a boss to get involved with her employee, after all. We both know that. And besides, you're still not sure you're going to stay past summer. Better to keep things on an even keel and just remain friends."

"Yeah, right. I get it. So all that sweet talk last night was just for show? All that talk about taking things slow and us having a chance, was all of that just your way of trying to draw me out and get me to talk, Stella?"

Stella thought about throwing chunks of bread at him. Or maybe an egg or two. "No, *I* meant what I said and I'm not trying to trick you into anything. But it doesn't really matter how I feel. You're not ready to be honest with me and I can't let things go any further unless you are. So in spite of what we talked about last night, we need to stay clear of each other before everyone around here has us paired off. We don't want people getting the wrong idea."

"No, and you sure don't want *me* getting the wrong idea, either. And you're obviously having second thoughts this morning." He gave her a direct look, his eyes drenching her in longing and need. Then he put his hands on his hips and tilted his chin. "But mark my words, Stella. Before I do leave this place, I'm getting that one kiss you owe me. So you'd just better get used to *that* idea, at least."

Before Stella could think of a quick retort, he was gone. She watched, her mouth still open as he stomped through the yard and slammed the back gate. Then she heard his truck cranking with an angry roar of engine.

"I don't get him," Stella said to herself as she went into the laundry room to fold the clean linens. First the man tells her he wants to take things to the next level in their relationship, but he also tells anyone who'll listen that he isn't ready for a long-term commitment and he isn't even sure he wants to stay here in Hot Springs anyway. Then he goes and gets all huffy with her simply because after hearing his conversation with Mrs. Creamer, she agrees and thinks it's wise to keep things on a professional, working level, even though last night was special and sweet.

But he stills wants to kiss you.

What could he possibly expect from her if he didn't even know what he wanted himself?

He expects a kiss, that little voice in her head reminded her. And you sure hope to honor that promise.

Stella sighed into the clean creamy-yellow towels that belonged to the Sunflower Suite. What would it be like, to be kissed by Adam Callahan?

After all, he was a handsome man. Rugged and a little hard-edged, but good-looking in that mystery man kind of way. He had a good work ethic, no doubt about that. He sure wasn't a slacker like her dearly departed Lawrence had been. No, sir. Adam was one of those men who just knew how to take care of things. He'd be good to any woman lucky enough to get him.

But…you don't want him, do you? And you sure can take care of yourself. She was using the excuse of him being honest to hide her own dishonesty—she *was* very interested in Adam Callahan. It wasn't right and it wasn't fair, but she and Adam both had some soul-searching to do before they could move forward.

It wasn't that Stella didn't want to get to know him better and maybe even consider him more than a friend. It was as though she was afraid to even think about that, afraid to expose herself to something she couldn't see or explain. It was just all too scary right now. She should have never teased him with the promise of more. Not even a kiss. Not even a touch. She should have kept things on a professional level. But last night… Forget last night, forget how he made her heart sing. Forget a future together.

She had a business to run, a son to raise, a sick daddy to take care of. How could she find any time for a love life anyway? That was just a silly dream, a lapse in good judgment.

She stood there in the sunny white laundry room, the scent of lemons and vanilla surrounding her as she held on to the fluffy towel, her crushed dreams as bright and full of hope as the sun's rays falling across the picture she'd hung there of an old farmstead with the laundry stretched across the clothesline blowing in the prairie wind, and she wondered why she felt like crying.

Then she heard the doves cooing, heard their babies chirping in the little nest cloistered there in the sweet honeysuckles and suddenly Stella understood.

She wanted someone to walk in the garden with her, someone to cuddle and coo with her. She wanted a helpmate, a soul mate, a partner. There was a tear in her soul and she wanted that tear healed and sealed up with hope and love and happiness. That wasn't such a bad dream, was it? Could she let go and have all of that with Adam, after all?

"Is it him, Lord?" she asked in a soft whisper. "Did You send this strange, intriguing, interesting man here to rescue me? Or to test me?"

For a minute, there was a sweet silence. Then a gentle, overwhelming thought popped into her head with such clarity, Stella wondered if the Lord had indeed spoken to her.

Maybe God had sent Adam to be rescued by *her*.

Stella heaved a shuddering sigh and wondered if

she could live up to that particular command. Or was she just chasing rays of sunlight in the middle of a summer morning?

## Chapter Twelve

Adam headed up the long main street into town, shifting the gears of his old truck as he left the hardware store on the outskirts of the city. He'd just been by the bank to cash his check and he had money to burn. Maybe he'd buy Kyle a set of those toy cars he liked so much. Or maybe he'd buy Wally a flash drive for his computer and show him how to use it to store information. Or maybe… No, he wouldn't buy Stella anything.

Because she'd just get the wrong idea. And because he was tired of her mixed messages. One minute she wanted him to kiss her and the next… well, he just needed to remember the woman's many moods and steer clear of trying to figure her out. But he couldn't get the image of her standing in that window out of his mind.

Telling himself he had to stay the course and relax, Adam said a little prayer. *I leave it in Your hands, Lord.*

Then he glanced over at the little art shop where they'd seen one of Estelle Clark's paintings. And before he knew what had hit him, Adam was parking and walking toward the open door of the shop.

The proprietor, a stout little man with a gray beard and a name tag that stated Richard Lampkin, grinned from behind the counter. "Good to see you, young fellow. It's been such a slow day, I was getting downright lonely. What can I do for you?"

Adam shifted back on his feet, then glanced around the long, narrow shop. "I'm looking for a certain painting by an artist named Estelle Clark—"

"Well, well," the man said, getting up to come around the desk, "you sure do have good taste, son. That is one of my prized possessions. It's right over here."

Adam followed the man to the back of the shop. "I want to buy it. I'll pay cash, but we need to do some negotiating. I don't have enough on me for the asking price."

The little man scratched at his beard. "You do realize an Estelle Clark painting is a rare find these days?"

Adam nodded as if he knew all about art. "So I hear. Why is that?"

The man scratched his bald head. "Well, we all knew her around here, of course. And while she was alive, she always sold real well at any kind of arts-and-crafts shows we'd put on. Then when she got sick, well, she couldn't participate so much. Of course, after she died, well, then everybody and his brother wanted one of her paintings. I had several in stock—I held them on consignment for her and we'd split the difference. Made a good bit of money that way. She had one fancy showing in a gallery just around the corner, too. Went pretty good."

"Why didn't this one sell then?"

"I can't explain that. The artist herself gave it to me just before she died, wouldn't hear of me buying it outright. Said to make sure I sold it to someone very special. But for some strange reason, it just hasn't gone out the door like I expected it to. I finally decided to just keep it—unless someone had a very good reason to buy it."

Adam decided this man sure was lonely. He seemed to want to talk. But Adam wasn't in the mood to chat.

"Why have you held on to this one for so long? You could have swapped it out, or sold it to an art dealer, right?"

The man touched a hand to the flowers on the canvas. "I guess I didn't push it enough, even with the low price. You know, it is the last one, so unless someone really knows art and knows about Estelle, I don't go into a lot of detail about my little treasure here. I set it out occasionally, but I don't make a big fuss about it. I'd sure hate to see it go. And like I said, it's the strangest thing. Almost as if this particular picture is just waiting for the right person."

Adam leaned close. "Well, I might not be the right person, but I'm buying it for her daughter, Stella. It kinda needs to be a surprise."

"Oh, well, now, ain't that interesting! We've all heard the rumors about that situation. Not a pretty thing, a mother leaving her child like that. But I tend to believe there are two sides to every story."

Adam was losing patience. "I'm not here to discuss Stella's personal life. I just want to buy this picture.

She saw it here a while back and I think she'd like to have it back where it belongs—in the Sanctuary Inn."

The man drummed his fingers on the glass counter. "In that case, I'll make you a fair deal."

Adam wondered at that, but the man did seem smitten with Stella's deceased mother. And he couldn't help being curious himself. Feeling guilty since he'd practically told Stella off because of her own curiosity, he asked, "What was she like?"

The man grinned. "Estelle? She was a sweet, quiet woman. Everyone loved her. She had that big old house but she rarely visited with her boarders.

That was part of her mystery. She was a bit of a re-cluse, I reckon. But when she entered a room, well, she sure lit things up. Depending on what kind of mood she was in, of course."

Adam didn't want to think about that. Why couldn't Estelle have shed some of that light on her daughter. Stella had obviously inherited her moodi-ness, though. "I need that painting," he said, shuf-fling through his stack of twenties. Then an idea hit him, clear as a bell. "And I might have some artwork you could take on consignment."

"You paint?"

"Not me, sir. But someone else I know. And not canvases like this. China painting."

"China painting? You mean, on plates and cups and such? That might go over pretty good with the tourists. They love anything hand-painted."

"Let's talk business, Mr. Lampkin."

The storekeeper gave him a shrewd look. "A man on a mission. I'm willing to consider part cash and part swap."

"I'll bring in a couple of teacups for you. And maybe some porcelain plates, too. You can price them and give the artist her part and the rest you'll earn back toward the price of this picture. How's that sound?"

"Sounds fair to me, depending on the artist. I need to know if it'll be worth my effort."

"Stella Forsythe—she's the artist."

Mr. Lampkin beamed. "You don't say. Well, don't that beat all?"

Adam knew he was treading on very dangerous ground, bartering some of Stella's artwork for this last painting of her mother's, but he couldn't stop himself. "I need the painting now, though."

Mr. Lampkin nodded. "Okay, son. You look honest enough. Besides wanting to give it to Estelle's girl, why is this particular painting so important to you, anyway?"

Adam smiled. "Because I just might have to trade it for a kiss."

The little man let out a cackle of laughter. "Well, I sure don't want to disappoint you then. Let's get down to business."

Stella came downstairs to find dinner sitting on the table. Resentment toward Adam colored her world until she saw her father and her son setting out plates and napkins.

"Where's Adam?"

Wally glanced up as she entered their private dining room. "He said he had some things to do. He grabbed a sandwich and took off."

"Really?" Stella tried not to worry or wonder what things Adam had to do tonight. And she wasn't going to fret just because the man had been avoiding her since she'd listened in on his conversation with Mrs. Creamer earlier. What did she care anyway?

"He said not to wait up, either," Kyle added as he slammed silverware onto the table. "Ready to eat, Mom?"

"I am. What did you two cook up anyway?"

"Just a casserole," Wally replied. "Chicken and vegetables with a mashed-potato crust. It's like shepherd's pie without the lamb. I reckon it's an Arkansas-type shepherd pie."

Kyle laughed at that. "Grandpa, you're so silly."

Wally made a face, then motioned for Kyle to sit down. He waited for Stella to do the same. "Let's say grace."

After they'd said the blessing, Stella looked at the bubbling casserole centered on the table. "Who taught you two to cook anyway?"

"Adam," Kyle replied before shoveling in a steaming mound of food. "He said this is so easy even—"

"Even I could do it," Wally interjected, giving his grandson a warning frown. "You just throw everything into one dish and bake it. Easy."

"I could have cooked dinner," Stella said. "It seems I never cook anymore. I got so busy with cleaning the upstairs rooms and checking the supply closet, I guess time got away from me."

"We don't mind," Kyle said, his tone a bit too joyous.

"I guess you don't at that," Stella said, smiling over at him. "I appreciate the help. I got all the upstairs rooms cleaned and ready for this weekend's boarders. And the Creamers won't be leaving until Thursday, so we need to show them special treatment. They've been very loyal to the Sanctuary Inn."

"They went out earlier," Wally said. "I think they were going to have dinner at the restaurant out near Lake Hamilton."

"I like Mrs. Creamer," Kyle replied. "She tells me funny stories about her dogs. They like to chew everything."

"Animals can be that way," Wally said. They enjoyed their meal, laughing and talking about everything from dogs to the upcoming summer camp Kyle wanted to attend out on the lake. Then Wally pushed back his plate and let out a sigh. "I'm mighty tired tonight. Think I'll watch some sitcoms, then turn in early."

Stella gave him a searching look. "Daddy, are you taking your medicine?"

"Of course I am." He patted her hand. "Now, don't go get all worried. I'm old, Stella. And that means I'll have good days and bad days."

"But are you eating right? Does this casserole have too much fat?"

"No, it doesn't. Adam made sure he got low-sodium vegetables and the chicken is all lean, white meat. It's all right, honey."

"I just want you to take care of yourself," she said as she got up to clear the table. "I'll do the dishes. Kyle can help."

Kyle bobbed his head and carried his plate to the sink, then rinsed dishes to hand to Stella. "Can I stay up with you, Mom?"

"Nice try," Stella said, shaking her head. "But you still have a few more days of school. You need to get your sleep."

Kyle made a face, but when his grandfather held out his hand to the boy, he took it. "I'll get him bathed and in his pajamas," Wally said. "We can read a book before I tuck you in and we say our prayers," he told Kyle.

Stella watched as they marched off together, one old and tired and one young and full of energy. Which left her standing here, loading the dishwasher, all alone and full of inner turmoil.

Then she looked out at her studio and saw a light on there. Did she forget to turn it off earlier? Finishing up the dishes, she looked around the tidy kitchen then headed out the back door, the scent of gardenias and magnolias merging in the quiet night air as she moved through the garden.

When she opened the door, she found Adam standing in the middle of her workshop, his hands on his hips and a guilty expression on his face. "What are you doing?" she asked, all of her emotions coiled and frayed.

"I…uh…I cleaned it up in here a bit and I… uh…made you some new shelves."

He had indeed cleaned things up. At first, she wanted to scream at him for messing in her space. But how could she do that when he'd only organized things so she could find her tools and brushes and paints? The entire place seemed a little brighter and much more cheery. The man had even put a potted plant in one of the high windows.

"Alcohol and turpentine are right here," he said, waving toward a neat shelf. "And olive oil and kerosene are on the next shelf. Your paints are over there, in order and by mixture. I didn't mess with your drawings or sketches. Or the stuff you've got all ready to go into the kiln."

"I can see that," Stella said, her voice just beyond harsh. She couldn't find fault with his handiwork. "Why did you do this, Adam?"

"I was restless. I needed something to do, is all."

She smiled over at him, wondering if they could get past last night and this morning and everything else standing between them. "So you ran out of things to do inside the house and decided to come on out here?"

"You don't mind, do you? I mean, I tried to keep things where you could find them."

She didn't miss the way he averted his eyes. He was still uncomfortable after their spat this morning. "I don't mind. I have to admit I did at first. I'm kind of picky about people messing in my stuff. But this looks very neat and tidy and I can find things just by looking up at the shelves. That should make my work go much better."

He put his hands in his pockets. "Good, then. That's what I wanted. To make your work go much better."

"Well, that was nice of you."

"I didn't do it to be nice."

"Then why did you do it? Really, why?"

He shrugged, looked uncomfortable all over again. "I thought maybe if you could come out here and relax you'd feel better about things in general."

"I just might," she said, wondering if she'd been so cranky that the man felt obligated to make things pretty for her. "Trying to soothe my savage soul, Callahan?"

"No. You don't have a savage soul. But I do think your soul is a bit bruised."

"I'm fine," she said, a shard of anger cutting through her even while his kind words tugged at her heart. "We got everything cleared up between us this morning. You don't need to be fixing *me*, understand?"

"I'm not trying to fix you. Just trying to make your life a little easier."

"So that's your job now? You fixed things in the Big Easy, and you can't seem to stop here in sleepy little Hot Springs, Arkansas?"

"You don't have to make it sound like that."

Stella hated herself for being so cynical and mean, but it was her only armor. "You're right. I didn't mean it to sound like a condemnation or a whine. It's nice to have someone fixing things for me for a change."

He came closer. "That's what I mean. You're so used to being the one in charge, I just thought maybe I could soften things up for you some. You know, prove to you that your work has value, same as anyone else."

Stella wanted to tell him that he had done just that. He'd softened things so much around here, made things work so much better—including her—that she wanted to run to him and cry tears of joy. But she had to refrain from doing that. After all, she didn't want to get too comfortable depending on him. "You're almost too good to be true, Callahan, you know that."

He was in front of her before she took her next breath, his hands on her arms, his eyes holding hers. "I am not that good, Stella. I'm just a man who had to find a change. I've found that change—for the better. I can't make any promises or declare any truths, except the ones I've already told you. I believe God led me here and... I'll be here through summer."

"Did He lead you to me?" she asked on a gentle whisper, remembering the clear nudging she'd had earlier when she'd felt the Lord guiding her. Wanting to test both his faith and that theory the Lord had planted inside her stubborn head, she asked, "What if God sent you here so *we* could give you a soft place to lay your head, Adam? What if He wanted *us* to be the ones to help you, to give you some rest?"

She watched as his eyes went misty there in the muted light. "Are you willing to do that for me? Are you willing to accept me the way I am right this very minute, flaws and all, just to give me some sort of solace, Stella?"

Stella knew he was asking her to take her own leap of faith. But she still needed answers. "When you question a criminal, don't you need evidence before you can decide his guilt or innocence?" she asked.

"Yes, that's how we do it," he replied, confusion coloring his eyes now. "But we believe a man is innocent until proven guilty."

"Right. But you lay out all the evidence until you have answers, don't you?"

"Yes, we do."

"And that's what makes a cop tick, right? I mean, you have to get to the bottom of a situation before you can make a decision or pass judgment?"

"Yes, but—"

"Yes, but you can't declare a man guilty until you feel sure you have enough information. And you can't say he's innocent until you can clear him with that information."

He pushed a hand down his face. "Okay, all right. Are you sure you're not a lawyer?"

"Nope, I'm not a lawyer. I'm just a woman who got burned pretty bad the first time around. I don't aim to let that happen again."

His arms held hers. "I'm not that kind of man."

"Then prove it."

"I thought I was doing just that. Haven't I tried to do everything around here you asked me to do?"

"Yes, and then some."

"But that's not enough?"

She backed toward the door, then put her hand on her heart. "They say action speaks louder than words, but I need to feel it here, Adam. Right here."

He came toward her, a frustrated frown on his face. "You are one stubborn woman, Stella."

"I've been told that, yeah."

"I don't know how to reach you."

She glanced around the studio. "Keep trying. I don't want you to give up on me just yet. In spite of how I protest."

That made him smile. "I don't plan on giving up, no matter how much you protest."

She turned to leave, then brushed a hand over the

clean worktable. "This really was awfully nice of you, Adam."

He followed her out. "Would you do me a favor then?"

She turned. "Oh, here comes the other part."

"There is no other part. I just want you to go to church with me on Sunday. Just try it. You might find some answers there, at least."

"I don't need answers from God, Adam," she said as she headed back toward the house. "I need answers from you."

"But God is part of what makes me who I am," he argued, stomping after her. "C'mon, Stella. What do you have to lose?"

She whirled on the steps, her face inches from his. "This," she said, her hand on her heart again. "If God sent you, then He'll just have to understand that I have to have proof that I can count on you in a pinch. You and Him."

Then she shut the door and left him standing there staring after her.

# *Chapter Thirteen*

Stella heard the church bells early on Sunday morning. It was a gray still day, with dark clouds hovering like a blanket over the mountain. The house was quiet. Everyone else had either headed out to explore the mountains or headed off to church with Adam. So that meant she was alone. Stella enjoyed having time to herself, but it was almost too quiet this morning. She'd never been one who needed the company of others to entertain her or validate her. But she couldn't help thinking about Adam and how spending time with him seemed to cheer her and make her smile, too. That is, when they weren't arguing about kissing and other such things.

He hadn't asked her again about going to church this morning. And even though she wouldn't have gone if he had asked, Stella felt a bit put off. Maybe he was getting the hint that she didn't feel comfortable in organized religion. Or maybe he was beginning to see that getting any closer to her was hopeless. She should be glad about that, not disappointed. After all, she'd held him at bay for weeks now, using the excuse of not knowing about his past as her only shield. But Stella knew her reluctance was about much more than Adam's past. More likely, it was all about her own past and her feelings of abandonment and her extreme lack of self-worth.

Adam Callahan was like the pied piper of religion, escorting his merry band of followers down one hill and up the next, past towering magnolia trees and blossoming crape myrtles to that little wood-and-stone church with the shining white steeple.

"I guess I should just tear out of here and join them," Stella said to the still air of the kitchen. Why did she always wind up here, staring out this window anyway? Why couldn't she just find something to do, or at least some other place to ponder all the thoughts whirling inside her tired brain? "But I might get caught in a storm."

She thought about going out to the studio, but not even that indulgence could entice her this morning. She'd probably just stand there at her worktable, staring at Adam's tidiness or at her mother's unopened trunk. She turned to find something to eat, then saw a tiny Bible lying on the kitchen table. *Kyle's.* Her daddy had given it to him last Christmas.

Stella picked up the white leather-bound book, her hand moving over the gold-etched lettering on the front. "You forgot your Bible, baby." She thought about running up to the church, just to hand the book to her son. But, no, that wouldn't work, would it? Then she might be forced to stay.

Instead, she dropped the Bible in her apron pocket, grabbed her cup of hot lemon-and-mint tea and put an oatmeal cookie on the saucer, then headed out back to sit in one of the old wrought iron chairs on the patio off from the house. The wind was picking up and because of the clouds, the morning was cool and pleasant. She'd sit out here and watch the storm roll in.

It wasn't until after she'd sat down that she realized she still had the little Bible in her pocket. "Well, I'm getting downright senile, not remembering things." She'd meant to put the book back in Kyle's room.

Stella put her tea on the table then stared down at the book. She did forget to bring the morning paper out. And she didn't want to have to get up and go and fetch it. Maybe she'd just glance over the Bible. She knew all the stories, of course. But it had been a very long time since she'd taken the time to read any of the passages.

Her mother had read her Bible stories when

Stella was very small, but then Estelle had become more and more involved in her art and less involved in her church or her daughter's life. As the years passed, the task of keeping the faith had fallen to Stella's father. And once Estelle had left, even Wally had fallen behind on that duty.

"I reckon it can't hurt," she said, her voice carrying loud enough to scare a squirrel down the trunk of the old oak tree. Thunder rumbled off in the distance, scaring the tiny creature even more.

"Excuse me," Stella said, laughing at the skittish little varmint.

She sipped her tea, then thumbed through the Bible, letting her fingers land where they might.

"Hebrews."

Stella sat quiet, then gasped at the verse she found. "'Now faith is the substance of things hoped for; the evidence of things not seen.'"

She held her breath, her hand on her beating heart as she read the passage over again. This was the verse she couldn't remember, the verse that had passed through her head just the other night as she'd sat on the bench waiting for Adam.

Was this a sign?

How many times had she hoped in her secret heart that Adam might be the one for her? How many times had she prayed to the God to whom she was so afraid to turn, asking Him to show her a sign of faith?

"I guess this is a *sure* sign," Stella said, taking a bite of her cookie. Then she shook her head. "Okay, so I turned to that particular passage. Big deal. Nothing to be seen here. Nothing to read into, anyway. I just happened to touch on that passage, is all." Then she thought about the passage again—"the substance of things hoped for, the evidence of things not seen." Maybe there *was* a lot to be seen in that particular verse. She'd remembered part of it, but there was a lot more written in that simple declaration. A whole lot more.

The little squirrel fussed up in the tree. The wind picked up again. More dark clouds started forming back behind the mountaintop. Apparently, it was going to rain sooner than she'd thought. Off in the distance, she heard a siren whining through town, its shrill alert growing closer and closer.

Then Stella heard a sharp hissing sound and the fluttering of wings and birds shrieking.

She turned to see a big black-and-white cat running through the yard.

With a baby dove in his mouth.

"Oh!" Stella threw the Bible on the table, her chair skidding as she sloshed tea all over her apron. "You mean old cat, let that baby go!"

One of the adult doves fluttered around on the ground near the cat, acting as a diversion for the baby.

"Let it go!" Stella screamed, her hands flapping to mimic the valiant bird trying to save the baby.

The skittish yard cat dropped his prize and took off running through the hole underneath the old gate. Stella rushed to the hurt little bird, tears welling in her eyes. "Oh, poor baby." She didn't know if she should touch the tiny bird or not.

Wiping at tears, she watched as the mother dove fluttered and fussed. "What should we do, Mama?" she asked the frightened dove.

To her amazement, the feathery baby hopped toward the mother. Thinking maybe the baby was okay, Stella glanced at him. She saw a little trickle of blood near the tiny bird's neck. But before she could reach out to help it, the little bird lifted in flight toward the thick protection of the honeysuckle bushes. The mother dove flew right behind it.

Taking a deep breath, Stella sank back on her knees, tears streaming down her cheeks. She didn't know why she cried so hard, sitting there all alone in her garden, the first fat drops of rain hitting her. She only knew that something deeply imbedded inside her heart had opened like a raw wound as she'd watched the mother dove trying desperately to fight for her baby.

And then, suddenly, Stella knew why she was so upset, why watching the doves had so moved her.

Her own mother had never fought for her like that.

Stella looked up at the clouds floating by in the blue-gray sky, the rain coming as fast as her own tears. "Why, Lord?" she said on a rusty whisper. "Why did she do that to me?"

The only answer Stella heard was the thunder off in the distance and the gentle cooing of the mother dove, calling to her fledgling.

Adam came running up to the house, out of breath and soaked to the bone. He had to find Stella. But when he saw her sitting on her knees, crying, he was afraid to tell her what had happened.

"Stella?"

She turned at the sound of his voice, her tear-streaked face full of both awe and fear. Quickly wiping her eyes, she asked, "Adam, what are you doing back so soon?"

Adam bent down beside her, ignoring her question for now. "Are you all right?"

She nodded, took the hand he offered. Her skirt was wet and muddy, her eyes swollen. "An old alley cat tried to get one of the baby doves."

Adam pulled her up, then stood close as he steadied her. "I'm sorry."

"The baby got away, because the mother fluttered and fussed, me right along with her. We scared the cat and the baby went into the bushes. But could you check on it for me?"

Adam wanted to do that, but he had to tell her. There was no way around it. "Later, honey. Right now we need to get to the emergency room."

Stella backed away from him, her eyes full of confusion and dread. "Why? What happened?"

"It's your daddy. He—"

She stepped back, shaking her head. "No, don't you tell me that, Adam. My daddy was just fine this morning."

Adam held her steady, but he felt the tremors moving over her body. "He started having trouble breathing just as the service started. We called 9-1-1 and an ambulance came. They got him stabilized, but we need to get to the hospital."

"No," she said, shock coloring her face in a pale white. "No, this can't be happening." Then she gasped. "I hear a siren. I heard the ambulance."

"C'mon," Adam said. "I'll drive you to the hospital. He'll probably be just fine by the time we get there."

"But he's not well," she said as Adam guided her toward the house. "He's not well, Adam."

"I know, I know," Adam said. "We just have to pray that the doctors can figure out what happened."

The look on her face scared him. She didn't want to believe in prayer. "Do you think God will save my daddy, Adam?"

"I can't promise that," he said as he watched her

turning off lights before she grabbed her purse. "But I'll tell you this." He pulled her close, his face inches from hers. "No matter what happens, *I'll* be here, Stella. I can promise you that."

She didn't answer him. Instead, she whirled and headed out the door toward his truck, her hands clutching her big shoulder bag. Adam decided he'd have to do all the praying for both of them.

Stella paced the small waiting area outside the emergency room at the nearby hospital. She was cold and wet, and she couldn't stop shivering in spite of the clean blanket a nurse had brought her. "Why aren't they telling us anything?"

Adam sat in his chair, watching her. "We'll know soon, I hope."

"Are you sure Kyle is okay?"

"I just called the Creamers," he said, "and he's fine. They took him to a fast-food place after church. Now they're back at the house. Mrs. Creamer is manning the phones and the check-in desk, too."

"We don't have anyone coming today, that I know of," Stella said, her voice vague and scratchy. "I got a call yesterday about a wedding later in the summer, but nothing else—" She stopped, pushed at her hair. "Adam, I can't stand this. I'm going to find a nurse."

He was up and in front of her before she hit the doors, his hands reaching for hers. "Now, just hold on. You just harassed the nurses five minutes ago. Let 'em do their work, okay?"

She gave him a murderous look, then sank down in a vinyl chair. "Okay."

Her quietness was even more worrisome than her frantic ranting when they'd first come inside the emergency-room doors. Adam wasn't sure what would happen if her father got worse or didn't make it. Stella might not ever forgive herself or God, for that matter. He didn't know how to console her, so he sat still and prayed for the right words.

He sat down beside her, afraid to touch her, afraid to talk to her. If he did or said the wrong thing, she'd shatter right before his eyes. Stella pretended to be strong, but Adam knew differently. And he so wanted to break through to that tender heart deep inside her pain.

He wasn't prepared for her tears. When he heard her sniffing, he touched a finger to her chin. "It's gonna be all right."

"You can't promise me that, so don't even try."

"No, I can't promise you anything, but you just have to have faith—"

She turned on him then, her eyes heated with disbelief and anger. "Have faith that God will make things right? That He'll take care of my son and me?

Have faith that even if I die old and alone, God will be there waiting on the other side of all my misery? I'm sorry, Adam, but I can't see that right now."

"You're worried and upset," he said, thinking he was pushing the envelope here. "Just try to relax and…ask God for some help."

She put a hand over her mouth, then whispered, "I've been doing that since the day my mother walked out on us. But…I don't think God is listening to my pleas." A sob shuddered through her. "I guess some of us just aren't worthy of that kind of attention, that kind of peace."

Adam took her hand in his. "You are worthy, Stella. God doesn't play favorites. If he did, I sure wouldn't be on the list."

She sniffed, pushed his hand away. "Don't give me that. You were—are—one of the good guys, Adam. You worked to help people down in New Orleans."

Adam felt his own anger boiling red-hot. "I wasn't a hero, Stella. You want to know why I left, why I haven't talked to anyone in my family very much since I came here? And why I don't want you to know about all of that? Well, I'll tell you. I found out one of my brothers was doing something illegal and I tried to cover for him. He's a plumber and construction worker and he was doing some price gouging on the side after the hurricane. I turned a blind eye because I loved him. It got both of us in hot water. I didn't have the courage to arrest my own brother, but I should have. Now, half my family is not speaking to me because I didn't arrest him and the other half isn't talking to me because I came clean and told the truth after he got caught. I had to walk away from my job and my life, all because I was trying to protect someone I loved. So don't ever think I'm some sort of hero or good guy. I'm a human being and I made a bad mistake. And that's why I don't want to talk about it."

He stopped, saw the shocked expression on her face but he was so tired and weary, he was beyond caring. "I'm sorry. You wanted to know what I'm running from. Well, I guess I've been running from myself."

## *Chapter Fourteen*

Stella stared at the man across from her, the impact of his confession chilling her to the bones. This certainly wasn't how she'd wanted Adam to open up to her, but since he'd blurted the whole story out, she intended to keep him talking. "You're ashamed because you tried to help your brother?"

He shook his head. "I didn't help him. But when I found out what he was doing, I didn't turn him in. I should have. But he's my brother. And he promised to stop the price gouging immediately."

"Did he?"

"Yes, but it was too late. Somebody else turned him in. I had to watch as they booked him into jail."

Stella could only imagine how Adam had been torn by his decision. No matter what he did, someone would wind up hurt. She thought of the tiny baby dove and the mother fighting to save it. "So why did you have a fight with him? I mean, if you weren't the one who turned him in?"

"But I knew, Stella. I knew what he'd done and I kept that information to myself, to protect him, to protect our family. That goes against everything I've ever been taught in life. And it went against my job. I've never been dishonest in my work, but this…this hit me in a bad way. My daddy practically disowned both of us. But my mama, she's a bit more forgiving. She was disappointed, but she never once turned against us."

"Did you get fired from your job?"

"No. I resigned a few days after I told the chief the truth. He didn't want me to quit, but he certainly understood."

Stella wanted to reach out to him, but her emotions were too jagged right now, and they both were too vulnerable at the moment. It would be a mistake for both of them. "So you just left."

He nodded. "I drove away and I didn't stop until I got here and stopped right at your door."

She let the significance of that fact sink in. He'd never lied about that, at least. He'd never lied to her about anything. Now she could understand his need to keep his past private. He'd been protecting his family, especially his brother. Hadn't she and her dad done the very same thing after her mother had left? They'd tried so hard to protect each other. "What happened to your brother?"

Adam lowered his head then rubbed his hand down the back of his neck. "He had to pay a fine and he's doing community service and he's on probation. As long as he keeps his cool and doesn't backslide, he'll be okay. He's actually helping to rebuild down there, but this time for free. He wants his baby boy to be proud of him."

Stella could understand that concept. "Sounds like he learned his lesson."

"I think he did. He's young and he was influenced by the wrong set of friends. But me, I don't have that excuse. I just turned a blind eye out of some misguided sense of duty and loyalty."

Stella touched her hand to his arm. "Adam, you love your brother. You were hurt by what he did, and you wanted to protect him. Maybe you used bad judgment, but your intentions were honorable."

He got up to pace, then whirled to look down at her, his next words full of sarcasm. "Yeah, my intentions are always *so* honorable, but this time my sense of honor forced me to leave my home."

"You didn't have to leave. You could have stayed and worked something out. *You* didn't break the law."

"I might as well have. People look at you differently when they find out you've withheld information. It's hard to find anyone's trust after that. That's why I didn't want you to know."

Stella saw the torment in his eyes. "I think I trust you even more now, for telling me the truth."

His head came up, then he let out a long sigh. "Then I'm glad you know the truth. Maybe we can just get past that now. I don't have any more secrets, Stella."

Stella wanted to get past all of her own doubts and fears, but she was too worried about her daddy to think beyond this hospital. However, she could offer Adam some hope. "Your secret isn't so bad, Adam. My husband did a lot worse than that. He lied, cheated and stole without batting an eye. He cleaned out our savings and wasted the money away on ridiculous schemes and empty promises. So don't feel like you're alone in your embarrassment."

He sat back down beside her, then took her hand. "But you wanted complete honesty from me. You think I'm that kind of man, the kind who is always on the right side of the law, the kind who does no wrong. Now you know, I make mistakes, same as anyone else. Sometimes the best of intentions bring about the worst results."

Stella nodded. "Yes, but I also know the difference is, you turn to God to make things right. Not just with the world, but within yourself. The rest of us could learn a lesson from that."

"Do you think God will forgive me?"

"Oh, Adam, I know that in my heart," she said. "I might not reach out to the Man Above for everything in my life, but I sure can believe that He's in your corner."

The look in his eyes held her. "Stella, if He can forgive me, why can't He do the same for you? And why can't you turn to Him now when you need Him the most?"

Stella couldn't answer that question, except to say, "Because I'm afraid I won't like the answers He might offer me. I don't want my daddy to die. I didn't want that little dove to die. That's why I'm afraid to even pray. I'll ask for something God can't give me."

Adam held her hand tight in his. "Listen to me. Prayer is not about getting our way. It's about letting God show us His way. If it's time for Him to take your daddy home, then as hard as that is to accept, we have to let go and know that God will be there waiting for our loved ones. It's a sad thing for those of us left behind, but a joyous thing for Heaven." He glanced out the window. The sky was still gray, but the rain had stopped. "We'd like to protect those we love forever, just like that mama dove. But we have to let go and know that some things are in God's hands. And sometimes we can't save the ones we love. Those little birds will leave the nest, no matter what we do. And their mother instinctively knows that."

"Is that what you believed when you left New

Orleans to come here? Did you just give up and let God take over?"

"I didn't turn my back on my family, if that's what you think. I went to my brother before I left and told him I loved him and that I wasn't leaving because of him. But he saw it differently. We had words, but he knows I love him. And my mother knows I might come home one day, whether everyone there wants to see me or not. So I reckon I did let God take over. I needed a break, and I found it here with you. But one day, I'll have to go back and face my family."

She started crying again, but this time it wasn't just for her daddy. Thinking about the mama dove, she asked, "What about my mama, Adam? I'm not sure where she stood, faithwise, when she died? I…I need to know if she made it into God's arms."

He gave her a long, measuring look, as if he wanted to tell her something. But he held back, then said, "I believe she made it, Stella. And I believe in spite of her actions here on earth, she loved you a lot. Maybe she was kind of like me and my brother. She did what she had to do, to protect you."

"But why couldn't she have been more like that mother dove? Why didn't she fight for me?"

"I think she did, in her own way. She loved you enough to let you go."

As her heart flooded with hope and understanding, Stella gave in to the need to pull him close. "You make everything seem so right," she whispered through her tears. "Even when it's all wrong."

Adam held her close, the warmth of his arms around her like a shield against all the ugliness of the world. Then he tugged her back in her chair so she could lean on him as they sat there in the corner, waiting on word about her daddy.

About an hour later, a doctor came out of the emergency room. "Mrs. Forsythe?"

"That's me," Stella said, jumping up. "How's my daddy?"

"Wally is just fine," the doctor said, a gentle smile on his face. "It wasn't a heart attack but it was a bad case of angina. We're going to release him, but he has orders to follow up with his heart doctor first thing tomorrow morning. I think we can adjust his medicine a bit and hopefully he won't have another scare like this."

"Are you sure?" Stella asked. "He's been so sick."

"I can't be positive, but I can offer you some hope. Of course, you have to consider his age and his medical history."

Stella nodded, unable to argue that point. "I'll make sure he gets to the doctor tomorrow. Can I see him now?"

"Of course. He's been asking for you. If you'll

just fill out some forms, you can visit with him while we wait for a wheelchair. Then you can take him home. Oh, and make him rest in bed all day, okay?"

"Okay." She turned to Adam. "I'll be right back."

"I'll bring the car around," Adam said after shaking the doctor's hand.

Stella nodded, then followed the doctor to the room where they'd put Wally. She stopped just inside the door, watching as her father's breath caused the hospital gown they'd put on him to flutter. *Thank You, God. I didn't want to pray because I only wanted to ask You to spare him. But... You knew that anyway. You knew how to hear my prayer, even when I couldn't voice it. And now I have to accept what I know in my heart, Lord. I can't control everything myself. I have to turn some of it over to You.*

Stating that prayer brought Stella a powerful sense of peace. It would be hard. Life was always hard. But if she turned to God, He could help her bear the worst of burdens. Maybe He'd been doing that all along.

Stella went to her father with a new presence inside her heart. No matter what happened, she believed that Christ would guide her father home one day. And Christ would also guide her through life, both the good and the bad. That assurance had been in her heart, right there where she'd hidden it for so long.

And come next Sunday, she would be the one to ask Adam to walk to church with Kyle and her.

\* \* \*

Things were different now.

Adam grinned as he surveyed the new and improved Sanctuary Inn Bed-and-Breakfast. The whole house had been painted a glistening bright white and the shutters were a dark green. The contrast made the old place look neat and pretty, and the scalloped white fringe around the eaves only added to the wedding-cake look of the Victorian farmhouse.

"Not bad, if I do say so myself," Adam said, turning to high-five Kyle.

"Not bad," Kyle mimicked, taking the same stance as Adam.

Now that school was out, the boy was like a little shadow, following him around, offering to help out. He'd helped out, all right. Kyle had more paint on him than he'd put on the part of the house Adam had allowed him to tackle. But that was fine by Adam. He was a happy man these days.

"Think Mama's gonna like it?" Kyle asked, his hands on his hips.

"I do believe she will," Adam said as he started gathering up their paint cans and brushes. "But she won't like it if we leave this mess in her flower bed. Let's get ourselves washed up and clean for dinner."

"She's making fried chicken."

"Can't wait for that."

"And you know somethin', Mr. Adam? I don't

think she's gonna burn it this time. She said she's learning to let things simmer, whatever that means."

Adam had to chuckle at that. He knew what it meant. Since the day they'd brought Wally home from the emergency room, something had changed inside Stella. And that something had broken all the walls she'd built around herself. Which made Adam happy. Very happy.

Stella was letting him get closer, each and every day. They weren't arguing or discussing anymore. They actually had quiet conversations about mundane little things. They were free and clear and… ready for anything. They enjoyed sitting in the garden with guests, or taking the long walk up toward town for some food and music. They'd even hiked up the mountain together for a nice picnic while Kyle was at day camp out on the lake, but only after a church friend had offered to sit with Wally.

In spite of her worries about her daddy's health, Stella was taking things much better these days. She watched out for Wally and made sure he went for his checkups and took his medicine, but Adam could see the peace in her face now. And she'd been going to church with him on a regular basis. That did his heart good.

She'd just been standing there one Sunday morning, waiting for him at the bottom of the steps in a pretty floral dress, her Bible in one hand and a dainty antique purse in the other. Taking Stella to church had been a big step. The climb up that hill had felt like climbing a mountain, but they'd done it together.

She'd also spent more time out in her studio, doing her china painting. He thought about the painting he'd bought for her. Her mother's painting. He was waiting for just the right time to give it to her, because there was a lot more to that still life than met the eye. A whole lot more.

He finished cleaning his brushes, then glanced up to find her standing there at the kitchen window, her smile indulgent and pretty. "Spying on us, Stella?"

"I can't help it if I happen to be standing by my kitchen window, now can I?"

"I reckon not. That chicken sure smells good."

"It's almost ready. And after we eat, we need to go over the details of the wedding. Only three days away."

"Okay. I finished the house just in time. Everything is ready."

Wally peeped around the window, grinning. "The first wedding at the new and improved Sanctuary. I sure hope the bride and groom are as spruced up as this old place."

"We'll make sure of that," Stella said, laughing. "I've got everything planned. Now, if the weather will just cooperate."

"Should be clear," Adam said through the window. "When are they due in?"

"Thursday," she replied, a dreamy look on her face. "The rehearsal dinner is set for seven at the seafood restaurant out on the lake on Friday night, then Saturday morning they get hitched right here in the garden. It's going to be so pretty. And it will bring in a pretty penny for the old Sanctuary."

Adam laughed at her pragmatic nature as he shook out the wet brushes then glanced around the backyard. The magnolia was in full bloom now and the pine trees swayed, their graceful broomlike green needles floating in the wind. The crape myrtles were blooming white and pink to form a perfect path for the bride to walk toward the gazebo. They'd set out chairs and tables they'd rented from a place called Majestic Tents and Adam had built an arbor and painted it white so Stella could plant a running rose that would one day cover the whole thing in delicate salmon-pink blossoms. Right now, it was doing its duty by blooming along one side of the arbor.

"I could get married here," he said, then he turned to find Stella still there, her eyes as brilliant green as the shutters. "Did you hear that loud and clear?"

"I did," she said, grinning. "Your dinner is going to be cold."

"I'm coming," he said. He whistled his way into

the house. He'd just hit the back door when his cell phone rang.

"Hello?"

"It's Richard Lampkin. How you doing?"

"I'm fine," Adam said, careful to keep his voice low. He hadn't heard from the art dealer in days. "How're you?"

"I'm good. Hey, I sold both those teacups and saucers you brought me. Got a pretty price. Enough to more than pay for what I gave up on that painting."

"That's great," Adam said, wondering what to do now. He hadn't told Stella about what he'd done.

"I need some more, son. I got customers asking for them."

"Uh, that might not be so easy." Adam glanced up to find Wally motioning him to dinner. "I got to go. I'll come by tomorrow and we can talk."

"Okay, but I'm serious. I think we're on to something here."

Adam heard the glee and the tad of greed in Mr. Lampkin's voice. He was thrilled that the shopkeeper had sold some of Stella's art, but Adam still had a big problem.

He hadn't found the right time to tell Stella that he'd taken some of her teacups and plates to Mr. Lampkin. He'd been waiting until her birthday, which was Friday. He'd planned a special dinner and he wanted to give her Estelle's painting then, and tell her about how excited Mr. Lampkin had been even before he'd sold her work. She'd need time to digest everything Adam wanted to say to her. But now he had to wonder if that had been wise, not telling her right off. Or worse, not asking her if she'd be okay with that. With all the excitement around her father's health scare, Adam had put off explaining his bartering with Stella. Now he'd have to explain why he'd kept it from her. Or maybe he'd purposely put it off, because he wasn't really sure of how she'd react and…well…he liked seeing her smile. He liked the new and improved Stella. He loved the complete, happy Stella. He just had to find a way to tell her all of this.

"Stupid," he said, hitting himself on the head.

Kyle gave him a sideways grin. "You talking to yourself, Mr. Adam?"

Stella lifted her eyebrows as he entered the dining room. "What's wrong?"

"Oh, nothing I can't fix," Adam said, hoping with all his heart that he could fix this. He sure didn't want to mess with the peace and quiet around here. And he didn't want to hurt Stella in any way. But he was so worried that he'd do just that, he didn't even get to enjoy eating her fried chicken. Which was a shame, since Kyle had been right. She hadn't burned it at all.

# Chapter Fifteen

Stella stood inside her studio, her gaze moving over the soft sun rays shining down from the high windows. She'd managed to get back into her china painting in a big way. The guilt was gone now. It had been replaced by a sense of accomplishment and peace. And today—her birthday—she hoped to get in some work before all the guests in town for the wedding returned from the rehearsal dinner late tonight.

Everything was set for the wedding tomorrow. The food for the early-morning wedding breakfast was prepared and tucked away, and the caterers would bring the cake and the food for the wedding early tomorrow. The tables and chairs they'd rented were set up out in the garden and Adam and Wally, with a little help from Kyle, had made sure the yard looked its very best.

The inn was booked solid, every room and suite filled by the bride's and groom's immediate family. The wedding had brought lots of people to other hotels and bed-and-breakfast spots in Hot Springs, too. A nice birthday present for a woman who just months ago had felt as if she'd bitten off more than she could chew with this place.

Stella felt a sense of pride all the way around. Her life was changing, day by day. And she had God and Adam Callahan to thank for that transformation. So she wouldn't think about the end of summer and the chance that Adam might go home to New Orleans. She refused to be negative or glum today. She wanted to pour herself into her work for an hour or two—a birthday present to herself.

And later, Adam had a special dinner planned. Or so he'd hinted all day.

Stella smiled at that as she went to the shelf where she kept her finished plates, her mind still reeling at *why* she'd changed over the last few weeks. Stella couldn't explain this change, but since the day she'd watched that mama dove fighting for her baby, she had found God again. Completely and without hesitation.

The events of that day—the trauma of watching that little bird suffer, coupled with the scare about her daddy's health, should have made her even more doubtful, even more angry at God. But she wasn't angry anymore; she needed God in her life. Somehow she'd realized that, sitting there, crying in the rain. If she couldn't have her mother's love, well, she could have God's love. He never abandoned people. The Lord was a lot like the doves. He fought for those He loved. Even those who sometimes abandoned Him.

Deep in thought, Stella moved her hands over her finished plates and teacups, her mind cataloging each one. Glancing back over the display, she noticed something was wrong.

"Something's missing," she said to herself. Maybe Adam had rearranged again. The man liked to organize things, that was for sure.

She checked and rechecked, but Stella couldn't find three of her prized teacups and matching saucers. Two of them had been done with delicate wisteria blossoms and vines trailing around the ridges, while the other one was from the Confederate jasmine collection she'd just started.

She'd have to ask Adam about them, she reckoned. Then she turned and saw that her mother's old trunk was also gone. "Now what has that man done?"

Confused, she glanced at her watch. Adam was at the hardware store, doing last-minute stuff. That's what he'd told her when he'd left about thirty minutes ago. She'd just have to wait until he got home to ask him if he knew where the missing items were. Or she could just go up to the apartment and check up there. Maybe he'd placed some of the stuff in the tiny storage closet at the top of the stairs.

Irritated that she was wasting time, Stella couldn't stop herself from going up to look. She reached the top of the stairs and opened the storage closet. Nothing there but a broom, some cleaning products and some of Adam's personal things. Did she dare go into the apartment?

*She did.* Stella's heart was pumping, a kind of dread mixed with anticipation rippling through her pulse. She didn't want to go into this apartment that her mother had used as a private retreat. But then, maybe this was the only way to break that last thread of resentment she still held for her mother.

She opened the door and glanced around at the tiny kitchen-sitting room. The long, sunny room looked clean and neat, all the dishes washed and stacked on a little drain, the dining chairs pushed up against the round oak table. Nothing here to prove he'd moved some of her pieces.

She was about to turn and leave when she caught sight of something in the corner behind the little love seat. An easel with an old blanket covering it. Had Adam taken up painting, too?

Stella had to smile at that. He'd done a great job on the house, at least. But she had to know what was underneath that old blanket. Then she gasped. What if this was something her mother had left up here?

Stella rushed to the easel and pulled back the blanket. Then she stood back and gasped again, her hand flying to her mouth. *"Awakening,"* she whispered. Last time she'd seen this painting, it had been at Mr. Lampkin's art shop on Central Avenue. Where in the world had this come from? And how had it wound up here?

Adam bounced into the kitchen. "Stella?"

No answer. Wally and Kyle had gone fishing with one of Wally's new church buddies to get away from all the earlier frenzy of getting the wedding group checked in and settled. And the group would be gone the rest of the night, so Adam knew Stella was alone in the house. They had a few hours before the wedding party came back from the rehearsal dinner at the lodge out on the lake. That gave Adam time to make Stella a good dinner then present her with her birthday present…and tell her about the success of selling her teacups. He hoped she'd be as pleased as he was, and he hoped this would be the jumping-off place for her to pursue her talent.

He hoped.

Quickly putting his groceries away, he called out to her again. No answer. Maybe she was out in the studio.

\* \* \*

Stella heard Adam calling her name downstairs, but she couldn't move. Why did he have her mother's painting? And why was her mother's old trunk now back up here, shoved behind the love seat?

She sat in a dining chair, staring at the morning glory and the cardinal. What did this picture mean anyway? Both the bird and the flower looked surprised at the discovery of each other. It didn't make sense to Stella. Suddenly, after feeling so at peace all week, nothing seemed to make sense. She felt that old familiar sensation of not being in control. Had she just imagined her new contentment? Had she just imagined that she might have a future with Adam? He'd told her he didn't have any more secrets, but he'd been hiding this from her. Why?

She heard his feet hitting the stairs and turned just as he came into the room. Pointing toward the painting, she asked, "Adam, what's going on?"

Adam looked from Stella's confused face to the painting, then back. No use in trying to keep it a surprise now. The look on her face told him that he'd messed up, big-time.

"I…I wanted to give you this tonight at dinner. For your birthday."

She looked shocked, then relieved. "You bought this for me?"

"Kinda," he said. "I need to explain—"

"What do you mean?"

He could see shards of the old stubborn, hurt Stella in her green eyes. "I mean, I wanted to cook you a nice meal, and give you something special for your birthday. But you found the painting."

"Yes, I found the painting," she said, getting up to place her hands on the table. "But I came up here looking for some of my art pieces. And I have this funny feeling you know where my china pieces are, too."

Adam took her hand then guided her back into her chair. Pulling out the other chair, he sat down. "That was part of the surprise. I, uh, I had to barter with Mr. Lampkin to get the painting and since I was sure he'd like your pretty little teacups, I suggested he just take a look at a couple of them—"

She shot out of her chair, her eyes wide. "You did what?"

"I took some of your work to Mr. Lampkin—just a couple of teacups and matching plates. And, Stella, he loved them. He sold them right off the bat and asked for more. I thought that was a good sign."

He could see the shock and anger in the flush moving down her face. "You thought that was a good sign? You just took it upon yourself to steal my stuff and pass it off so I could have this painting back?"

"I didn't steal anything," he said, rising up to glare down at her. "I took a couple of teacups, as samples. I didn't know the man would sell them right away."

"You didn't know because you didn't stop to think. You didn't bother to ask me how I'd feel about this, either." Pushing past him, she shouted, "All I asked from you was honesty, Adam. In all things, honesty. And I had actually begun to trust you, to…love you. But you had to go behind my back and ruin everything." Then she pivoted at the door, tears falling down her face. "I don't want that painting, and I sure don't want to trade part of my soul just to have it or you. I want both you and it out of here by morning. You don't need to barter for me ever again."

With that, she was gone down the steps, leaving Adam standing there in the middle of the still, sunny room. He turned to stare at the painting, wishing he'd at least had the chance to tell Stella the significance of her mother's legacy.

Stella got up at six the next morning, her eyes puffy from crying and lack of sleep. Before she could finish washing her face, Kyle came bursting into the bathroom.

"Mama, why is Mr. Adam's bags all packed up and in the back of his truck? Where's he going?"

Stella swallowed past the lump in her throat. She hated to disappoint her son yet again, but it couldn't be helped. She patted her face with a towel, then turned to face Kyle. "Mr. Adam has to go back to New Orleans."

Kyle's bottom lip trembled. "I don't want him to do that. I want him to stay here. He promised he'd show me how to throw a baseball. He promised."

Stella closed her eyes. "He promised me a lot, too, baby. But he has to go back and see his family. They miss him."

"We'll miss him more!" Kyle turned and ran out of the room. Then she heard him telling her father that Adam was leaving.

Hearing her son's sobs coming from the next room just about did Stella in. She could hear Wally's whispered response, but she was crying too hard to make out what her daddy was saying. She sank down on her bed, holding her stomach, her own tears hot on her face. Was she being unreasonable asking Adam to leave? On the one hand, he'd done a noble and honorable thing, buying back her mother's painting. But on the other hand, he'd gone about it the wrong way. If only—

Stella wiped her eyes, determined to put dreams of what might have been out of her mind. She had a wedding to get through. In about three hours, her yard would be full of people who'd come to Hot

Springs for a joyous occasion. She had to prepare herself and her home for that. And afterward, she'd cry about Adam Callahan and how much she'd miss him.

Adam watched as the bride and groom drove off in a vintage car, headed to the airport to start their honeymoon. The last of the guests would now load up and go home. The wedding was over and the happy couple would soon start a new life together.

A new life. He'd thought he'd found that here, with Stella and her family. It was going to be so hard to leave them. He should have left before daybreak, but he wanted to stay and see that the wedding at least went off without a hitch, even if his own life had hit a brick wall.

And he had one more thing to do before he left.

So with determination, he turned from the cluttered tables and trailing streamers left over after the wedding reception and started toward the kitchen. He was going to have it out with Stella Forsythe, once and for all. If he left mad, at least it would make the leaving easier.

He found her standing at the kitchen window, staring out into the garden. Adam took a stance right in her line of vision, digging in his heels until she noticed him.

"Spying on me again, Callahan?"

Her words didn't have that spunk he'd come to know and love. Her voice sounded strained and forced.

"I'm not spying, Stella. We just need to talk, is all."

"I'm done talking."

"So you're just gonna keep standing at that window, looking out, hoping for the life you refuse to allow for yourself?"

She looked him square in the eye then. "It's my window and my business. And your time here is up."

"Not just yet," he said, coming so close he could see the flecks of brown in her green eyes. "My time here isn't nearly up. And if you'd just listen to reason—"

She pinned him with another frown. "There is no reason for what you did. You went behind my back. You talk about being noble and honest, but you still like to do things your own way. Maybe that's what got you in trouble down in New Orleans in the first place—" She let out a gasp, then put her hand to her mouth, regret coloring her eyes. "Adam—"

Her words pierced Adam with all the clarity of a knife cutting into his heart. "Don't," he said, his breath coming too quickly. "You wanted me gone, then I'm gone. But you need to go up to that apartment and look at that picture, Stella, really look at it. And you also need to read the letters your mama left in that old trunk. Letters to you, Stella. That was the real gift I wanted to give you last night."

An hour later he was on the outskirts of town when his cell phone rang. The caller ID showed the number for the inn. At first, Adam ignored the ringing phone. He wasn't going back to the Sanctuary Inn. But the phone kept on ringing, so he snarled a "Hello."

"Mr. Adam?"

"Kyle, is that you?"

"Yessir. We need your help. Grandpa and me."

Adam pulled into a fast-food joint, then stopped the truck. "Kyle, is Wally okay?"

"He's fine, except something went bad wrong out back. The water sprinklers you installed a few weeks ago went all haywire. Now there's water everywhere and Mama's out there, all wet and we can't get the sprinklers to shut off and, well, she'll have to pay for the damage to the tables and all. There's pink from the ribbons on the white cloths. It's a mess. Can you come and help us, please?"

How could Adam turn down that innocent plea. "I'll be right there, Kyle."

He did a U-turn then headed back toward the inn. He'd fix the problem, then he'd be on his way home. After all, he was so very good at fixing things.

\* \* \*

Stella stood in the middle of the garden, tears falling softly down her face. She couldn't get the sprinklers to turn off and the leftover wedding cake and food was ruined, right along with the once-white tablecloths and the ribbons of pink satin the rental place had provided. She'd have to pay to have it all cleaned or replaced.

But she didn't care. She was crying because she had just made the biggest mistake of her life. She'd let the man she loved go, without even fighting to keep him.

And all because of her resentment toward her mother.

Wally came running out to tug her into his arms. "Honey, you're getting all wet."

"I don't care," Stella said. "Daddy, I'm so sorry."

"For what, sweetheart?"

"For never understanding." She wiped at her eyes. "I understand now. I saw the painting. I read the letters."

"You're not making any sense, sugar. C'mon into the house and let's get you dry."

"I can't," Stella said, wishing she could tell Adam how sorry she was and how much she loved him. But she'd sent Adam away. He'd tried to be noble and do the right thing, but she'd accused him of just the opposite.

She'd seen it all right there in the painting. There embedded in the flowers and leaves just below the surprised morning glory had been a message from her mother.

"To Stella, love Mommy."

Those precious words were hidden there, curled around blossoms and entwined with vines. And to back them up, letters in the old trunk, stacked neatly and bound by a blue ribbon. Letters to Stella that stretched over years and years, telling of her mother's struggle with mental illness and how she'd had to seek help, telling of Estelle's fear that she couldn't be the best mother to her little girl. So…she'd let Stella go, left her to the stable, hard-working father who could take care of her. Estelle had died all alone and away from her family, because she was too afraid of being a burden.

Things hoped for. Things not seen.

Her mother had left her a message, going on faith that Stella would know Estelle loved her.

Why couldn't Stella have gone on faith, with her mother and with Adam? And why wouldn't these aggravating sprinklers cut off?

He found her standing there, all wet and shaking her head, her long hair hanging down to her waist, her pretty blue dress ruined and clinging to her in soaked tufts of watery silk.

"Stella?"

She turned to stare at him, then blinked. Then she started crying again. "Adam, you came back."

"The sprinklers," he said, walking through shooting water to get to her. "Kyle called me."

Stella's sobs grew louder while Adam grew wetter. She shook her head. "Great. Another man with honorable intentions around here."

"You need to get out of this water," Adam said as he went to the main line for the sprinklers and tried to turn the stuck valve. With a good wrench and a little grunting, he finally got the thing shut off. The cascading water went from an all-out hissing and swishing to a gentle spew and then finally, to tiny little trickles around the yard.

Adam waited until the water died down, then went back to stand in front of Stella. "It's over. I fixed it."

She looked up at him, watering dripping off the crape myrtle trees all around her. She had several tiny pink blossoms scattered like a veil in her hair. She gulped back a sob and said, "I love you, Adam. Can you fix that?"

Adam looked into her eyes and saw the truth shining there. "You do?"

She bobbed her head. "I do. I'm sorry I got so angry about the painting. It's the nicest birthday gift I could ever have."

He pulled her into his arms. "You saw the picture?"

"I saw," she said. "She left me a message."

"She sure did. And she left you the story of her life, too, Stella. Did you find the letters?"

She pulled back to nod. "Yes. I read them and now I understand so much more about her. There was always so much more to her than we could see."

"I'm glad you see now," he told her, pulling her back into his arms. "I'm so glad for you."

"Will you forgive me, then?"

"Only if you'll forgive me."

She smiled, then wiped at her eyes. "I think we have a deal, Callahan."

Then he backed away, his hand moving down the tear streaks on her cheek. "I have to go home, though."

She looked confused, but he lifted her chin with his fingers. "I have to make peace with my family, Stella, so that when I bring my bride to meet them, they won't turn me away."

She started crying again. "You want to marry me?"

"I sure do, and soon." Then he tugged her back into his arms. "But before I leave to fix this one last thing, you owe me something."

"What's that?"

"A kiss." With that, Adam held her head in his hands and leaned down to touch his lips to hers. He savored the sweetness of her mouth, the salt of her tears and the smile he felt coming from inside her soul.

Then they heard giggling and both turned to find Wally and Kyle at the kitchen window, watching them.

"Are y'all spying on us?" Stella asked, her hand in Adam's as they strolled through the wet grass toward the house.

"Yes, ma'am," Kyle said, grinning from ear to ear. Then he glanced around to his grandpa. "We saved y'all some wedding cake, before we turned on the sprinklers and tightened the spigot, I mean."

Adam grinned, then put his arm around Stella's shoulder. Giving her a look that told her all that was inside his heart, he said, "Wedding cake. That sure sounds nice."

Stella smiled up at him. "Yes, it does."

With that, he lifted her up in his arms and spun her around and around, laughing as he kissed her again.

And off near the honeysuckle bushes, the gray doves lifted their voices to coo their gentle approval before they spread their graceful wings to fly away home.

\* \* \* \* \*

*Don't miss Lenora Worth's*
*next Inspirational romance,*
*A FACE IN THE SHADOWS,*
*available May 2008*
*from Love Inspired Suspense.*

Dear Reader,

The mountains of Arkansas are a beautiful reminder of God's enduring love. These mountains remain a constant throughout changing seasons and centuries of civilization. That is why I wanted to set a book in this particular part of the country.

It was challenging to have two very different characters fall in love, but I knew from the moment Adam stepped up on Stella's porch that God would help me figure out the details. Stella had forgotten that sometimes, no matter how much life knocks us down, we have to go on faith. Adam had seen the worst of life, but he'd held on to his faith. He was a perfect example of God's enduring presence in times of trouble.

I hope you have faith in things unseen and that you know God loves you, even if you might not always feel His presence. Look for sanctuary in His arms. I hope you enjoyed watching Stella and Adam fall in love. You can write to me through my Web site at www.lenoraworth.com.

Until next time, may the angels watch over you always.

*Lenora Worth*

## QUESTIONS FOR DISCUSSION

1. Why was it so hard for Stella to go on faith? Do you find it hard to do so yourself at times? Why or why not?

2. How did Adam use his faith to overcome his pain? Does your faith help you to work through times of crisis?

3. Why was Stella so afraid of losing her father? How did Adam show her that God would help her through her father's death?

4. Why did Kyle act so mature for his age? Do you know of children who have to take on adult responsibilities? How can you help them to just be children?

5. Do you have a special place that you consider a sanctuary?

6. How do you turn to God even when your faith is shaky? Do you believe God can show you the way even when you can't see Him there? Why or why not?

7. Why did Stella resent her mother? How did Adam help her to overcome that resentment?

8. Do you believe a person should use his or her gifts as a witness to God's grace? How did Stella learn this lesson?

9. What did Adam do to ruin the trust Stella had in him? What was his biggest flaw?

10. Do you see nature as part of God's presence in your life? Is nature important to your faith? Why or why not?

# REQUEST YOUR FREE BOOKS!

## 2 FREE INSPIRATIONAL NOVELS
## PLUS 2
## FREE
## MYSTERY GIFTS

*Love Inspired*

**YES!** Please send me 2 FREE Love Inspired® novels and my 2 FREE mystery gifts (gifts are worth about $10). After receiving them, if I don't wish to receive any more books, I can return the shipping statement marked "cancel". If I don't cancel, I will receive 4 brand-new novels every month and be billed just $4.24 per book in the U.S. or $4.74 per book in Canada, plus 25¢ shipping and handling per book and applicable taxes, if any*. That's a savings of over 20% off the cover price! I understand that accepting the 2 free books and gifts places me under no obligation to buy anything. I can always return a shipment and cancel at any time. Even if I never buy another book, the two free books and gifts are mine to keep forever.

113 IDN ERXA   313 IDN ERWX

| | |
|---|---|
| Name | (PLEASE PRINT) |
| Address | Apt. # |
| City | State/Prov. | Zip/Postal Code |

Signature (if under 18, a parent or guardian must sign)

### Order online at www.LoveInspiredBooks.com
### Or mail to Steeple Hill Reader Service:
**IN U.S.A.:** P.O. Box 1867, Buffalo, NY 14240-1867
**IN CANADA:** P.O. Box 609, Fort Erie, Ontario L2A 5X3

Not valid to current subscribers of Love Inspired books.

**Want to try two free books from another series?**
**Call 1-800-873-8635 or visit www.morefreebooks.com**

* Terms and prices subject to change without notice. N.Y. residents add applicable sales tax. Canadian residents will be charged applicable provincial taxes and GST. This offer is limited to one order per household. All orders subject to approval. Credit or debit balances in a customer's account(s) may be offset by any other outstanding balance owed by or to the customer. Please allow 4 to 6 weeks for delivery. Offer available while quantities last.

**Your Privacy:** Steeple Hill Books is committed to protecting your privacy. Our Privacy Policy is available online at www.SteepleHill.com or upon request from the Reader Service. From time to time we make our lists of customers available to reputable third parties who may have a product or service of interest to you. If you would prefer we not share your name and address, please check here.

LIREG08

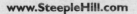

*Love Inspired*®

# TITLES AVAILABLE NEXT MONTH

## Don't miss these four stories in April

### DRY CREEK SWEETHEARTS by Janet Tronstad
*Dry Creek*

They'd parted when his career took off, but musician
Duane Enger was back—and determined to win back his
high school sweetheart. Linda Morgan wasn't sure she wanted
to pick up where they left off, though Duane was the one person
who could make her heart sing.

### HER BABY DREAMS by Debra Clopton

The Mule Hollow matchmakers were at it again, and this time
they had Ashby Templeton in their sights. Despite her hopes of
a family, she couldn't believe Dan Dawson was the right choice.
The flirtatious cowboy was determined to change that—and
make Ashby his bride.

### A COWBOY'S HONOR by Lois Richer
*Pennies from Heaven*

Gracie Henderson's husband Dallas had been missing for six
years. Now he was found, but robbed of his memory by a tragic
accident. Gracie was relieved to have answers, but she had to
protect her child. Could a rekindled love heal her doubts?

### MILITARY DADDY by Patricia Davids

They'd made a mistake that had led to an unexpected blessing:
Annie Delmar and Corporal Shane Ross were to become parents.
Shane wanted to be part of his child's life…and part of Annie's.
But getting Annie to give him a second chance would be the
greatest battle he'd ever faced.